I0817956

not like she thought

(an ilse beck fbi suspense thriller—book 5)

ava strong

Ava Strong

Debut author Ava Strong is author of the REMI LAURENT mystery series, comprising six books (and counting); of the ILSE BECK mystery series, comprising seven books (and counting); of the STELLA FALL psychological suspense thriller series, comprising six books (and counting); and of the DAKOTA STEELE FBI suspense thriller series, comprising three books (and counting).

An avid reader and lifelong fan of the mystery and thriller genres, Ava loves to hear from you, so please feel free to visit www.avastrongauthor.com to learn more and stay in touch.

ISBN: 978-1-0943-9418-3

BOOKS BY AVA STRONG

REMI LAURENT FBI SUSPENSE THRILLER

THE DEATH CODE (Book #1)
THE MURDER CODE (Book #2)
THE MALICE CODE (Book #3)
THE VENGEANCE CODE (Book #4)
THE DECEPTION CODE (Book #5)
THE SEDUCTION CODE (Book #6)

ILSE BECK FBI SUSPENSE THRILLER

NOT LIKE US (Book #1)
NOT LIKE HE SEEMED (Book #2)
NOT LIKE YESTERDAY (Book #3)
NOT LIKE THIS (Book #4)
NOT LIKE SHE THOUGHT (Book #5)
NOT LIKE BEFORE (Book #6)
NOT LIKE NORMAL (Book #7)

STELLA FALL PSYCHOLOGICAL SUSPENSE THRILLER

HIS OTHER WIFE (Book #1)
HIS OTHER LIE (Book #2)
HIS OTHER SECRET (Book #3)
HIS OTHER MISTRESS (Book #4)
HIS OTHER LIFE (Book #5)
HIS OTHER TRUTH (Book #6)

DAKOTA STEELE FBI SUSPENSE THRILLER

WITHOUT MERCY (Book #1)
WITHOUT REMORSE (Book #2)
WITHOUT A PAST (Book #3)

CHAPTER ONE

Adelaide looked at herself naked in the full-length mirror, trying not to frown. She turned one way, then the next, tilting her head and studying her form. She forced a smile, flashing dental-strip whitened teeth, her scalpel-sculpted cheeks turning up.

Her nose didn't bunch like it used to when she smiled. She held the expression for a moment, turning again in the reflection. Small blue fairy-lights outlined the mirror, and the pinpricks of light reflected off the metal bar of the clothing rack behind her.

Someone knocked on her trailer door, a hollow, tinny sound. A voice called, “Ten-minute warning! Ten-minute warning!”

“Almost ready!” she called back.

But Adelaide made no move to get dressed. Something was still off... She couldn't quite place what. Her doctor had fixed the way her nose bunched when smiling, but now... She leaned in, her breath fogging the glass, the blue fairy lights bright in her eyes. She could just about make out the scars beneath her breasts as she leaned in—though she'd had multiple laser treatments to remove the evidence of plastic surgery.

Work had been done on her eyes, her nose—twice, her cheeks... That was only the beginning. Standing there, examining herself, Adelaide didn't see the same thing others did.

Her memories were too strong for that.

She reached out a finger, tracing it along the mirror, faintly, not wanting to smudge. The glass was cool against her skin. Her hair was still somewhat damp from the shower. Her towel lay in a puddle near the trailer door. The window behind the clothing rack was open, cracked. She didn't mind if someone looked in and saw her.

In fact, she quite liked it.

How many years had she been short, fat, ugly little Addy... Thank God her family came from wealth. She'd had her first corrective surgery at the age of fourteen. Slowly, but surely, over time, she'd grown quite beautiful beneath a surgeon's scalpel.

So what if they stared?

She could hear the sound of the voice from earlier, shouting nearby, through the window. "Ten-minute warning, everyone! Cameras, are you ready?"

She smiled now, the first authentic one in a while.

Cameras. She never would have guessed as a child she'd one day find herself in front of cameras for a living. From short, dumpy, and ugly, to a fashion model. This would be her second photoshoot—but jobs were lining up now. Her dreams were finally coming true.

She stared into the mirror, smiling radiantly, and doing her best not to see the many, many flaws that still needed addressing.

Oh well... One step at a time, she supposed.

She turned from the mirror, towards the clothing rack, reaching for the outfit the director had chosen for the day's shoot. Quite skimpy, with frills and lace more than fabric. But she'd worked for her body—the sort of body that put other women to envy, and men to lust.

She didn't mind flaunting it occasionally.

She heard a quiet tap on the window behind her, and she frowned without looking back. "I said I'm coming!" she yelled.

Then, she heard the sound of the window sliding open. She stiffened, standing naked and exposed in the mirror. She glanced in the reflection and her eyes went suddenly the size of saucers.

A man in a ski mask was climbing through her window. His head dipped under the sill, one hand braced against the cheap wood, holding it up. His legs already straddled the divider, and the fellow was already half inside the room.

For a moment, Adelaide didn't believe her eyes. She just stared at the intruder, mouth unhinged, goosebumps erupting across her bare skin.

Then, she began to scream. At the same time, she spun on her heel, sprinting towards the door to her trailer.

But the man was quicker. He lunged *through* the clothing rack, sending jackets and a couple of Gucci purses scattering. He tackled her around the waist, bringing her to the ground with a painful *thud.*

She gasped, trying to draw breath to scream again, but his hand—gloved in thick leather—scrabbled for her lips, holding her mouth sealed. She tried to shout again, kicking and bucking her hips, but he jammed his fingers into her cheek, sending a blossom of pain across her face.

His thick body stifled her, pinning her to the ground.

She tried to scream, to speak, to bite the fingers against her mouth, but he was too strong. He held her for a moment, panting on top of her, his knees pressed to the ground on either side where he sat on her stomach, holding her down.

With her free hands she was beating and scratching at the man's chest, but he ignored the blows as if they were little more than branches in the wind.

His chest heaved in a faint sigh as he exhaled at the ceiling as if offering up some silent prayer. Then, his ski mask tilted, his head with it, his eyes blazing from the gaps in the course cloth as he stared at her.

He held a gloved finger to his lips, his other hand still gripping her cheeks.

She tried to bite him again and this time managed to score a nip. He huffed, jerking his hand back in pain. She let out a strangled shout, but the sound was cut off halfway as he smothered her face with a hand again.

He leaned in now, adjusting his hips and slipping his other hand towards his waist.

Her stomach jolted; she felt a surge of terror. But the horror only increased as she watched him draw something long and sharp from his belt.

A knife. A wicked, curved blade like some prop in a movie.

He tapped the knife against her nose, the cold metal chilling her skin.

"No more screaming," he whispered, his voice hoarse. "Promise?"

She swallowed but nodded hurriedly.

He withdrew his hand, and she went still, staring up at him. Did she recognize him? No—no she'd never seen him before. Unless... Fear flared, and she let out a yell. "Heeeelp!" she screeched.

He slammed his hand back. His eyes blazing behind the mask. "You promised," he snarled.

And then the knife flashed down. She felt a sharp, jolt of pain in her chest. Her eyes bugged; this time, he released his hand again and she tried to shout. But the pain blossomed through her bosom, along her side. She tried to gasp for air, but it wouldn't come. She tried to speak, but she had no breath left for words.

"Sorry about your lung," he murmured, tapping a bloody knife against his lips, leaving a smear of red across the skin visible in the hole of the mask. "But it isn't right to lie. Liars don't get a happily ever after, do they?"

Her eyes fluttered, pain exploding through her abdomen. Hot, white lances of agony twisted her body. She tried to shift, to screech, to move, but none of it mattered. Her strength was fleeing. Sticky, wet warmth spread down her bare stomach.

"Good princess," he whispered above her. "What a lovely face... you cheated, though. Didn't you? Cheating, lying... Tut tut." He had an almost musical, sing-song quality to his words now. He tapped her on the nose again in a playful sort of gesture.

And then brought the knife flashing down once more. This time towards her face.

CHAPTER TWO

Barcelona. Dr. Ilse Beck had come so far, and now she stood with her back to the Sagrada Familia—the sacred family. An old church, though not *that* old given European history. The same church that had been in the brochure she'd found, the same Sagrada Familia her father kept babbling about back in his German prison.

"I told you I could get us inside," the tour guide was saying, his expression mischievous where he stood on the small, marble bridge over the mild stream. The faint sound of babbling water drifted over the buzz of pollen bees swarming the tulips in the garden beds.

Ilse studied the tour guide, glancing back in the direction of the old church. It was nearly a quarter mile in the distance. It had taken her a week, five visits and six tours to finally find a lead.

She looked back at the tour guide standing against the manicured landscape of the private garden. A manor settled the center of the landscaping beyond them both. A small, silver gate settled the edge of a tall hedgerow—the gate was now open thanks to the key in the tour guide's hand. He stepped along the marble bridge, pausing in the center and waiting for Ilse to join him.

The man was handsome, though a good ten years her senior. Ilse felt her insides churn with guilt as she studied the fellow. She hadn't been on a date in...

Well, ever.

This didn't count. Not really. The tour guide thought so, but it was the only way she had thought to get him alone. To ask him what she needed to. Granted, she hadn't *said* it was a date, she'd simply asked to be shown the private gardens he'd mentioned on more than one occasion while circling the old church.

"Well," Sergi said, quirking an eyebrow on his tanned skin. "What do you think?" he spread his fingers in a flourish to indicate the beds of tulips and trimmed rose bushes as well as the wooden sculptures set throughout the garden.

"It's beautiful, just like you said," Ilse replied, shifting uncomfortably and brushing her coal-black hair in front of her maimed ear.

“It's too warm for that,” the man said, waving towards her sweater. “Relax, allow yourself to breathe.” He flashed his million-dollar, Colgate smile.

Ilse tried to return it but left her sweater exactly where it was. She was sweating beneath it, but sweaters, sweatpants and the like were a staple of her wardrobe, and the only way she ever felt comfortable to venture out in public.

She didn't have pierced ears, nor did she wear makeup. Yet, in the past, she'd been told she had a sort of natural prettiness—not quite beauty, as her features were too youthful despite being in her early thirties. But men had shown interest in the past.

She'd simply never had the nerve to take them up on their offer. Besides, she refused to be so selfish. Dragging a poor, unsuspecting fellow into the nightmare that was her subconscious would've only caused pain.

Now, though, she'd made somewhat of an exception.

“This isn't a date,” she said, voicing her internal thoughts out loud. “I—just to be clear. I don't want to lead you on.”

The man on the bridge waved away the protest, snorting and turning to study the water. “Yes, yes, whatever you Americans like calling it, hmm? A one-night stand, huh?”

She winced. She'd never had one of those either. “No—I really meant it. I just need to speak with you.”

“You wanted to see the gardens, si?”

She glanced towards the flower beds and back. “I wanted to speak... to ask you about... about who gave you that.”

The man turned, frowning at her and watching where her finger pointed towards his throat. He swallowed, a rasping, guttural sound, causing the thin, white scar to rise and fall with the motion.

“You asked me to take you here to show you my scar?” he said, sounding mildly annoyed now.

“No—to tell me about the woman who gave it to you. You said she came on the tour a couple of years ago. The German woman.”

This, of course, was why Ilse had come all this way. She was on the hunt, just not for a man. Her stepmother, the woman who'd controlled her father, who'd manipulated Gerald Mueller. The true source of the horrors in that basement in the small, house hidden in the woods.

Ilse could barely remember the woman—she was a grayed-out memory in Ilse's subconscious more than anything. She didn't even have a name.

Yet.

But that was why she'd come to Barcelona, after all. And this tour guide had his own story... She'd heard it mentioned in whispers. And she'd arranged to speak with him in private to find out just how useful his information might be.

The tour guide turned on the marble bridge, extending his arms and resting his hands against the top of the rails. "Truly," he murmured, "You're here over my scar? That's why you kept coming to my tour? Five times?"

"Six, actually," Ilse murmured. She winced apologetically. "I didn't mean to lead you on. I just needed to speak with you alone."

"And we're alone," he said, raising his eyebrows hopefully.

"Not for... not like that...," Ilse took a step onto the bridge, but maintained her distance, the fragrance of the flowers a redolent reminder of fresh air and perfume. "I... I had wanted to ask you in the break room. But there were so many people around. I didn't realize the church employed so many tour guides."

"I see. Well," he said, his tone somewhat harsher now that the prospect of getting Ilse out of her sweater was rapidly diminishing. "What about it? I don't have all day." The warmth bled from his voice, replaced rapidly now by a frigid chill.

In part, Ilse had wanted to isolate the tour guide, to speak with him alone. But also... this was the garden the tour guide had been navigating two years ago during *the incident.* Only in whispered hushes and murmurs among the other guides at the church had Ilse heard anything substantial.

She'd traced the stories, listened to anyone who would speak. It had been crazy to come to Barcelona on a hunch. She knew that. Crazy to think in only a week she'd be able to find her stepmother.

But crazy sometimes met coincidence in a marriage of convenience.

"They... they say she was German," Ilse pressed, studying the scowling man. "They say she was middle-aged, and she had a knife when she attacked you. Is it true she was from the Black Forest?"

"Who told you that?" snapped Sergi.

"I—I just heard."

"It was Elena, wasn't it? That gabby bitch."

"Look—I just need to know if it's true... What happened?"

"Like you said," Sergi snapped, waving a hand and pushing off the rail of the bridge. "It happened years ago; I barely remember."

"Only two years. They said she tried to kill you."

“Hah! She threatened me. Not killed.”

“So it did happen!” Ilse exclaimed. “And was she German? Did she come from Freiburg near the Black Forest, like they said?” The same town her father was from. The same town near where they were keeping him incarcerated. Only rumors, so far, pieced together over time. It had all started with an offhand comment from one of the other tour guides. After Ilse's third visit, the tour guide had said, “Another German frequently visiting. I hope you're not going to try and kill Sergi as well!”

The guide had said it as a joke, but Ilse had questioned the woman about the comment.

Another German woman, two years ago, had visited the church. Had come nearly every day. And then... according to the rumors, had attacked Sergi Vlachos. The woman, it was rumored, had also been from Freiburg. A small town, not known for international travel. The odds were so slim...

“I don't remember. It doesn't matter anyway.” Sergi was now brushing past her, and moving back towards the small, silver gate in the hedge, his disgust clearly visible in every hasty footfall.

“Please,” Ilse said, keeping her distance, her feet solidly planted on the bridge. “I need to know.”

He glanced back at her, frowning, standing near a tall bed of red tulips. He turned, scratching at his neck absentmindedly, and shrugging. “It was two years ago. I won't remember much.”

“The woman in question,” Ilse said, “was she German?”

“Yes. So what?”

“And she was from Freiburg?”

“I don't know that.”

“Elena said she was.”

“Ha! So it was Elena!”

Ilse rested her hand against the cool, dusty marble railing. “That's not the point. This woman—what did she look like?”

“She was old. Maybe fifteen years older than me,” Sergi said with a shrug. He began to turn, moving towards the silver gate again. Only now did Ilse hasten after him, stray pebbles skipping as she hurried down the garden path.

“What else!”

“I don't know,” he snapped. He'd reached the gate now, and held it open, gesturing for Ilse to step through. “It isn't nice,” he said, “to get a man's hopes up, you know.”

"I never said it was a date," Ilse returned, rubbing at one arm and hunching her shoulders as she slipped back out onto the asphalt driveway.

"The two of us in a private tulip garden... A man doesn't normally think you're going to ask about a crazy lady attacking him."

"So she *did* attack you?"

"Barely," he scoffed. "I was fine. She barely hurt me."

"What about the scar?" Ilse pointed.

He snorted, turning and marching up the driveway now, back in the direction of the Sagrada Familia.

"Sergi," she called, "Please. I wouldn't ask if it wasn't important."

"The lady wanted my keys," he retorted back. But continued moving away from her. "I refused to give them. She threatened me with a knife. So I gave them."

"That... that's all?"

"No" he snapped, whirling around near the bumper of his car. "Not all. She then used the keys to sneak into the church at night. I nearly lost my job."

Ilse winced sympathetically. "Why did she need to go into the church."

"Oh?" he looked suddenly surprised, his eyebrows arching. "Elena didn't tell you that? Psh—typical."

Ilse frowned. "Why was she in the church?"

"To kill herself, of course. They found her body the next day in the belfry."

Ilse gaped. "They—they *what*?"

"She killed herself," Sergi repeated, eyes narrowed. He opened his car door, holding it apart as if braced against some unseen force. "Burned herself alive. People could hear the screams in the streets. They found her burnt corpse in the morning."

"I don't believe you," Ilse said reflexively. "It's not possible. She can't be dead."

"She is. They found her body. Look!" Sergi lifted his phone, typed something then jutted it towards her with a motion like swatting a fly.

Ilse stared at the headline—which had been translated roughly into English. *Woman Self-Immolates in Sagrada Familia.*

She read the first paragraph, her eyes gaping, her fingers trembling where they rested on her upper thighs.

Woman found burnt in the Sacred Family church of Barcelona. No identification discovered. Police rule it suicide...

Her eyes skipped to the next paragraph, but Sergi seemed to have had enough. He yanked his phone back, jamming it in his pocket, shaking his head. "Now—this has been a thoroughly unpleasant experience. Thanks for nothing. Probably best you *walk* back." He slipped into the car, slammed the door, and refused to look in Ilse's direction.

For her part, she stood, stunned on the asphalt, gaping after the man.

It wasn't possible. She didn't believe it. Her stepmother had killed herself two years ago? It didn't make sense... None at all. But if not a suicide, what? Whose remains had been found in the church? Why had her father's mistress been here at all in the first place?

Ilse blinked and only realized then that the car was peeling away from the drive leading up to the old manor and the manicured gardens. She stared after the retreating car, the angry taillights glaring, as the tour guide returned in the direction of the church.

Her stepmother had assaulted the man. Stolen his keys. Then... then someone had died, burned, in the church.

But it couldn't be her stepmother, could it?

Who was sending her those postcards? Who was the one taunting her with tchotchkes from her past? Someone who knew her name...

Her father? She'd already determined it couldn't be him. At least, not him alone. Someone was helping Gerald Mueller.

She'd assumed she'd find the answers in Barcelona.

But now... now she faced another dead end.

Ilse let out a painful little sigh of frustration. She stared across the old roads, in the direction of the Sagrada Familia.

There'd been nothing sacred about her own family. Nothing at all.

She'd come all this way for nothing. She'd been absent from her new apartment for more than a week now. There were only so many days she could take off from work.

Would there be another package waiting for her when she got back?

If so... her stepmother *had* to still be alive. Or else her father had been acting when she'd visited him in prison. Someone, something from her past was haunting her.

But the dead ends kept piling up.

She couldn't see through the haze or ash.

Would there be another taunting message back at home? Perhaps she wouldn't find what she'd need in Barcelona. She'd research the death, of course... But how far would that take her? Her mind wandered towards another potential connection.

Would there be a postcard waiting for her? Maybe she'd spooked the sender... Maybe this would all be over soon.

Or maybe it was just getting started.

CHAPTER THREE

Ilse's eyes were heavy as she pushed through the apartment door to her building. In one hand, she held a folded, lined piece of yellow notebook paper, upon which she'd copied the article online word for word. It hadn't been a very long article. Mostly due to the lack of details.

A burning victim in the old church. No ID, no DNA match. Ruled a suicide.

On the sixteen-hour flight, Ilse had combed through the notes, allowing her imagination to wander. To think like her father, like her stepmother for a change.

But none of it was clear. Had her stepmother faked her own death? Had she murdered someone? Had she really killed herself?

If so... who was sending the taunting postcards?

Ilse couldn't take much more. She knew an impasse when she found one. For now, she folded the notepaper, sliding it into her pocket and checking the main door to the building with her hip, allowed it to close behind her.

A cool gust of morning air swirled through the unit. She hadn't slept particularly well on the plane, between attempts at memorizing her notepaper.

But also, she'd been kept up with apprehension.

Would there be another note? Another doll?

She moved to the mailbox, her keys shaking in her hand as she opened the receptacle and peered into the darkness. With the same shaking hand, she reached into the mailbox. The keys, looped over her pinkie, clacked against the metal.

She pulled out a stack of bills...

Ilse stared at the bills, feeling a chill sense of relief. She sifted through the three envelopes... Nothing. No postcard. No...

She frowned, glancing back towards the open mailbox.

A fourth envelope was stuck under the lip of the metal lid. Momentarily, Ilse stared. She dabbed her tongue against the inside of her dry lips, her fingers curling as if in protest against her waist.

Then, unblinking, she reached for the envelope and pulled the letter from inside her mailbox.

She dropped the bills. They scattered like leaves to a forest floor.

"Damn it," Ilse murmured beneath her breath. She inhaled slowly, staring at the familiar handwriting looping the back of the envelope. "Schizotypal personality disorder. Borderline personality disorder. Psychotic disorder. Dahmer. Blonde hair. Ninety-four. Seventeen victims. May twenty-first," She recited beneath her breath, using the memory device to calm her nerves.

Ilse had something of an encyclopedic knowledge where serial killers, their victims, and their psychoses were involved. A morbid fascination to some, but crucial in her line of work. At least, her usual line of work. Recently, she'd grown more and more involved with the agency.

Now, though, her focus had zeroed in on the envelope. Her rising sense of apprehension was rapidly replaced by a stony countenance. She scowled at the offending piece of parchment, and with shaking fingers, slowly tore the envelope.

As the paper ripped, her hands grew steadier, her eyes narrower, the faint huffs of breath regularizing.

And there it was.

Another postcard.

This time from Barcelona.

"Shit," she muttered, staring at the old church on the front. The Sagrada Familia. This time, on the other side of the postcard, her tormentor had simply left a little smiley face and a single name. *Hilda.*

She stared at the image for a second, her heart pounding, and then she snarled, ripping the thing to shreds and scattering the pieces on the ground. She turned, marching up the stairs, ignoring the litter discarded behind her.

Whoever was taunting her wanted to make this *her* problem. But it wasn't. It was their problem, and soon, it would come with consequences.

Ilse just didn't know *how* yet.

She marched up the stairs, hands at her side, rather than holding the railing. Her eyes were still narrowed, and she refused to glance back towards the small, bits of ripped paper.

They knew she'd been in Barcelona. Whoever was taunting her, whoever was sending those postcards. Was it her father after all? Had she been mistaken? Or had his mistress faked her own death in the church for some unknown reason?

One of them, or both of them, were taunting her. Hounding her from her past.

The tragedy of the Muellers, the *curse* as some of her family members spoke of it, still haunted their lineage. Heidi was dead. Deirdre also gone in a car crash, Timothy was in prison, Hans and Dietrich dead from her father's rage after Ilse had escaped from the house. And little Kat was in an insane asylum.

And now the curse of the Muellers wanted to come for her as well.

But she refused to let it.

Her father couldn't reach her from prison. Her stepmother was either dead as well, or somewhere in Europe. Ilse was safe...

So why send the postcards?

What were they playing at?

Ilse reached the door to her apartment unit, pulling her keys from her pocket and feeling a rising sense of anxiety as she did. She felt prickles along her spine and shot a quick look down the hall. As she turned, she winced, feeling the faintest soreness along her side from the burns she'd received two weeks before.

She'd been in a hall then, too.

She'd been attacked.

But no one was there. The postcards were nothing. Ghosts were trying to haunt her, but none of it mattered now. As Ilse pushed into her apartment, her phone began to buzz.

She frowned, lifting the device, and then cursed.

A tele-conference with one of her patients.

"Dammit...," she kicked the door closed with her heel, latching it. Then, she winced, feeling a familiar sense of unease. She opened the door again, checked the hall, closed it.

But the unease remained. So she opened the door a third time, inhaled faintly, breathing long and reciting, "Brown hair. Brown eyes. Forty-two. Bundy. Thirty victims. Forty-six. November twenty-fourth." Then, with slower motions, she closed the door again.

Her fingers had steadied once more. Whenever it came time to speak with a client, she always managed to find a sort of inner peace. Not so much from herself, but rather on their behalf. They needed her strong, so she made herself strong.

She rubbed absentmindedly at her wrist tattoo which read, *Take captive every thought...*

With another, longer sigh, she tossed her bag onto the single couch and moved to the sparsely ornamented apartment's kitchen table. Her behemoth of a computer was set up there, next to the wood-burning stove beneath the analog clock.

Ilse hated technology. She turned on her computer and it began to boot up. It would take a few minutes to fully come to life. Even her internet was far slower than anything she experienced while working in the field.

Not that she minded. She liked a slower pace.

She glanced at her phone again. 9:58. Two minutes before the appointment. She felt a jolt of anxiety. If she was late, even by a minute, it would eat at her for the rest of the session. The *exact* time, the exact numbers mattered to her. Counting OCD was common, though not necessarily tied to trauma. In her case, it was often triggered by auditory cues.

She waited, sitting in front of her old computer, glancing towards the small, detachable web camera she'd purchased on the cheap when first moving into the apartment.

As she sat, her phone began to ring again. This time, though, not from the alarm or reminder.

She glanced at the phone, hesitated, looked at the clock. 9:59. She hissed but answered. "Make it quick," she said urgently. "I have less than a minute. Literally."

A voice cleared on the other end. Then, slowly, as if making a point, the even-keeled tone of Supervising Agent Rawley came over the device. "Doctor Beck," he said.

She didn't return the greeting, her foot tapping impatiently. Her computer had booted up now and with a sigh of relief she began navigating towards the video software.

"Hello? Can you hear me?"

"Yes, yes," she said, her lips pressing together.

"Ilse, we have a case," Rawley said. "We need you to come in."

Ilse clicked the video software, sending her client a link at the same time. She hesitated, only now registering his words. "W—now?"

"Yes. Now."

She let out a long breath. "I see. Umm... I have an appointment for the next hour."

"Can you get out of it?"

Ilse paused, glancing at the clock. 10:00 exactly. Suddenly, her screen sparked to life, and a second video feed appeared. Ilse smiled politely, waving to her client as the woman settled her headphones.

10:00 exactly. Punctuality mattered.

“I cannot,” she said swiftly. She smiled towards her client, wincing apologetically and pointing to the phone. Then, loud enough for her client to hear, she said, “Sorry, I have something *important.* I'll be there in a little more than an hour.”

Then, she hung up.

She wasn't sure why she did it so abruptly. It wasn't like Rawley had ever treated her poorly.

But in that moment, sitting in front of her computer screen, facing her client, Ilse wanted to focus on just one issue at a time. To focus on the woman on her screen more than anything. She didn't need postcards taunting her, killers needing to be nabbed—right now, she just wanted to help the single individual person in front of her.

Sometimes it was important to focus on the bad guys.

Other times, all she wanted to do was help their survivors.

Agent Rawley would have to understand. She'd been clear when joining the agency that she wouldn't forsake her clients.

She only hoped he'd understand.

Besides, an hour wasn't too long, was it? Things could be delayed an hour without causing harm

At least, so she hoped.

“How you doing, Dr. Beck!” A voice crackled from the speaker above her webcam.

Ilse kept her smile affixed, cleared her throat and said, “It's going well. And how about you?”

The woman in the video paused, seriously considering this question, her eyebrows bunching. For a moment, Ilse felt a jolt of guilt. Perhaps she should have taken more time to answer the question as well? How *was she doing?*

Perhaps not as well as she'd hoped.

But better than she'd been.

The same couldn't be said for the source of this new case. She glanced at the clock. 10:02. Only fifty-eight minutes left.

CHAPTER FOUR

Ilse was practically jogging as she entered the Seattle field office, springing off the elevator and moving down the hall into the large, cubicle-filled office space. She'd made sure her client hadn't felt rushed, but then she'd—much against the usual grain of her character—pushed the speed limit to reach the office.

Figures were moving about, and her gaze darted towards the large office at the back of the room, where she spotted an athletic figure behind a standing desk. She swallowed, staring towards Agent Rawley's silhouette, but before she could approach, a voice called from an open door in a darker portion of the hall behind her.

"Hey, Beck!"

She turned, glancing towards the small, utility closet which had been converted into Agent Tom Sawyer's office.

She glanced again towards Rawley, but the man wasn't moving, standing rigid like a statue, facing his computer.

With a sigh, she turned, moving in the direction of Sawyer's makeshift office.

Agent Tom Sawyer sat wedged behind a desk which was almost as large as the room itself, with barely a couple of inches between the left edge of the desk and the wall.

The lanky, thin-framed FBI operative was leaning back in his chair, his booted feet resting on his table, his legs crossed. He had a laptop on his jeans-clad legs and wore his flannel shirt buttoned to the top. His ever-present baseball cap was tilted back, revealing his uncombed, sandy hair jutting every which way towards the single lightbulb in the janitorial closet-turned office space.

The man studied his computer, his posture relaxed, except for his eyebrows above his green eyes. His face always had a stubborn look about it, even when he was on his own in the dark.

"Tom," she said, nodding in greeting. The last time the two of them had spoken, Agent Sawyer had revealed a piece of his own troubled past. A serial killer had murdered his sister. Sawyer still blamed himself to this day.

But now, as she watched him, he just looked up, mildly irritated.

"You're late," he said in his usual laconic way.

"Sorry about that. I told Rawley, but I had a client."

"Mhmm."

"Is... Is Rawley..."

"Pissed?"

"Yeah."

"Nah. Hard to get Rawley pissed."

Ilse nodded, brushing at her dark hair. *Unless you punch him, I imagine,* she thought to herself, remembering stories of Sawyer's own interactions with the field office chief. She still wasn't sure *why* Sawyer had once punched his boss. Nor did she understand why he was allowed back at the field office. But the reason for his cramped office space... that was plain enough.

"So..." she said hesitantly, "Rawley said there was a case?"

"Mhmm. Where you been?"

"Excuse me?"

Sawyer lowered the lid of his laptop where it glowed against his skin. He studied her, adjusting the brim of his baseball cap. "Where," he said, slower, "you been?"

"I—umm, on vacation."

"You weren't home."

"Right, like I said, I was on vacation—hang on, how do *you* know I wasn't home?"

Sawyer shrugged. "Stopped by."

Ilse blinked, staring at the man. She waited, expecting him to fill in the blanks, but he declined to do so and instead tilted the laptop lid again with a flick of his finger and resumed his study of the contents therein.

For a moment, she wondered if she ought to press the issue. Sawyer hadn't *stopped by* before. Had it been a social call? Was it something to do with a different case? Or had he wanted to talk about their last conversation?

"You know... I didn't tell anyone," Ilse said, cautiously, trying to read the man behind the desk. "About—about anything. I keep secrets for a living."

Sawyer looked at her, his lips pursed. For a moment, she thought he might be dismissive of this too. Nothing about his expression seemed vulnerable or emotive in any way. But instead of saying anything, he just met her gaze and gave the faintest of nods. So faint, she wasn't sure he hadn't simply shifted his head.

But then he glanced back at the computer. "Got a case," he said. "Been doing some reading while you were running late."

"I had a client."

"Right. Anyway, we got two dead."

He spun the laptop now and placed it on the top of his scarred and scraped desk. There were no ornaments, no pictures on this desk at all. It was just a hunk of wood for all intents and purposes.

Now, though, Ilse leaned in, her hands pressing the scarred wooden surface as she braced herself, peering at the images on the laptop.

She winced as she did, feeling her stomach turn. "How awful," she murmured.

"Yup. First one is the left. Second the right."

Ilse nodded vaguely to show she'd heard, but mostly she just stared at the coroner's photos. Both of the bodies had been brutally stabbed. There were gouge marks in their chests. In the case of the woman—though it was hard to recognize her as a female from the photo alone—her face had been punctured again and again.

"Is... is he using a knife?" Ilse whispered, feeling her stomach churn. She resisted a sudden urge to burp and instead turned away from the photographs on the screen, staring at Sawyer now, eyes wide.

Sawyer shrugged. "Looks like. First victim," his long finger tapped the left side of the screen from behind, "was a marathon runner. Stabbed in the lung, then chopped up—as you can see. The second," the same finger moved, tapping the right, "was a fashion model. Assaulted in her dressing room. No sexual motive so far."

"Sadistic, though," Ilse murmured.

"Come again?"

She pointed. "The first stab is to the lung according to the report here—am I reading that right?"

"Yeah, you are. What about it?"

"Well... it's measured, controlled. To work as a therapist, we do have some basic anatomy training. Taking the lung takes their breath, incapacitates them... Which then gives him the time to do the rest of... of this..."

"Hmm," Sawyer grunted. "So, you're saying he's a sadist?"

"With rage issues, yes. It starts out as a power thing," she murmured. "That's why the lung. But then... then he just...," she trailed off, staring grim-faced at the crime-scene photos.

"Loses control?" Sawyer ventured.

Ilse winced but nodded. "That's about right."

"Great," Sawyer sighed. "A sadist with anger management issues. Definitely the sort to stop after two, yeah?"

Ilse snorted, shaking her head. "We should be so lucky," she murmured. "No—no. If he's killed two, there's no reason to think he would stop now. Unless. Were the victims connected in any way?"

Sawyer reached over the lid of the screen now, tapping an arrow key. The browser tab shifted, and now Ilse found herself studying two dissimilar photos. The man's face was thin, athletic, not quite unlike Agent Rawley. His jaw was pronounced, his cheeks sharp. He wasn't handsome but wasn't ugly either.

The woman on the other hand was blonde, or at least pretended to be. She had a perfectly sculpted nose, cheeks, eyes. Everything about her seemed so... intentional. Like studying a first-year art student's rendering of a bowl of fruit. A bit too... perfect. None of the characteristic blemishes so often accompanying real life.

Ilse studied the beautiful woman—she was young, though it was difficult to tell from all the work that had been done. The man was middle-aged. He also had red hair. Arthur Lehman. She re-read the name beneath the file. She glanced at the woman. Adelaide Stevens.

"So they're not related?" Ilse said.

"Not family at least. But bodies were found in a twenty-mile distance."

"So pretty close to each other."

"Right. But no connection we found otherwise."

Ilse crossed her arms, nodding and studying the two pictures. Their healthy, smiling faces were so different than the first two photos she'd seen. Studying them now, she felt a jolt of grief.

How many of her own clients had escaped a similar fate by the skin of their teeth? What about Ilse herself? Most of her family was dead or in prison or insane. She'd somehow escaped. Barely.

Sometimes it was worth focusing on the survivors... Other times, it was about catching the bad guys so there were no victims to begin with.

"So we think it's the same guy for sure?" Ilse asked. "Because of the stab wound to the lung?"

"Yeah—seems so. Guy is bold too. The man was killed while on a jog in the middle of the afternoon. The woman was killed in the morning on a photoshoot set with people all around."

"I see. So sadistic, rageful, but also brash."

Sawyer nodded at her, slowly rising to his feet and closing the lid to his laptop. "Not a great outlook. But yeah, seems so. You good, doc?

Need more vacation days or wanna come with?"

Ilse frowned. She wasn't sure what he was implying, but a second later she caught the twinkle in his eye and realized he was just teasing. She flashed a smile, rolling her eyes. And though part of her felt the shared amusement, simply because she was fond of Sawyer, another part of her wondered at her initial reaction. She slipped back into the hall as Sawyer hopped his desk, slipping off the other side, and tilting his cap forward now. He smelled of sandalwood and sawdust. His stubborn green eyes studied her closely from beneath the hat.

"You good?"

She smiled again, this time less forced. "Yeah—where are we headed?"

"Second crime scene is freshest," Sawyer said. "Her trailer is still cordoned off—figure we can start there."

"Sounds good. Lead the way."

***

They were in Sawyer's vehicle this time, and Ilse kept shooting glances out of the corner of her eye towards the sandy-haired agent. He wasn't a very talkative sort. He'd often described himself as a man of action. He'd said he was married to the job.

But Ilse knew men like Sawyer. She'd spent time with them. There were millions of types of people in the world, but one reductive way to divide them: predators and protectors. She often had to fight the urge to think of everyone in those terms or as someone on the path to become one or the other.

Sawyer was a protector. And he hunted predators.

Now, as he stared through the windshield, his jaw tight, his eyes fixed on the gray roads swishing by as they moved through the Seattle city streets, she glimpsed his true nature just beneath.

She also, now, could spot the pain that was always there, lingering. The same sort of pain, of trauma she'd experienced in the past. The same sort of pain she'd often had to keep back with her own will and effort.

Now that she knew the source of it, Ilse wanted nothing more than to reach out and hug the man. Or at least to talk to him about it, to help him *feel* better.

"So," she said carefully, biting her lip. "How are you?"

He glanced at her, raised an eyebrow. Then looked back to the road.

“Constipated,” he said.

She blinked then he smirked and kept driving, picking up the pace.

Perhaps now wasn't the time... Sawyer clearly wasn't in the sharing mood. Still, her heart went out to him. But like Sawyer, while she wasn't a man, she *was* a protector too. The two of them had put devils behind bars in the past. Like guardian angels, hunting down wrongdoers.

Every time she received a postcard, received taunting from overseas, either by her father or at his command, it only filled her with an even greater sense of resolve to make sure men like him weren't allowed to continue harming others.

“Constipated,” she muttered. “Try prune juice.”

“Didn't know you'd take such an interest in my digestive system,” Sawyer quipped. “Hang on doc, we're merging.”

She gripped the arm rest, leaning to the side as he pulled sharply behind a truck, ignoring the blare of a horn, and then sped up the ramp, circling the Eastern front of the city, and moving in the direction of the set.

CHAPTER FIVE

They arrived at the crime scene and Ilse spotted two police cars sitting in the parking lot outside a large, warehouse-shaped studio. Two trailers sat on the lot, in the shade, beneath a green and white striped awning. A concessions table, laden with fruit, bottled water, sparkling drinks, and various snacks was visible just within the doors of the large set. A couple of figures were standing outside one of the trailers, next to the crisscrossing caution tape over the door.

The figures looked bored, and both of them wore the blues and blacks of Seattle's finest.

No one else was visible on the set, as if the studio had been, overnight, turned into a ghost town.

Sawyer pulled beneath a raised, parking lot bar, past a meter. A spot reserved for the handicapped sat off to the side, but Sawyer ignored this, trundling past and preferring to park in a spot further down the lot, even though no one else was on the scene. Sawyer was strange like this. Sometimes, he didn't seem to care about the rules at all, but when children or the injured or elderly were involved, he would follow the rules to the letter of the law.

She'd never seen him speed in a school zone, but she'd never seen him follow the limit on the highway. She'd never seen him be rough with a woman or an older witness, but she'd never seen him take it easy on a scumbag.

Now, as they came to a full stop in a parking space across from the handicapped spot, Sawyer put them in park, pulled the keys and flung open his door. "Ready, doc?" he called back.

She flashed a thumbs up.

The two of them moved around the hood of the car, heading towards the guarded trailer.

"Thing is five times bigger than my office," Sawyer muttered beneath his breath as the two of them moved across the asphalt. Stray pieces of gravel scattered beneath their feet. Ilse shifted, tugging uncomfortably at the sleeves of her sweater and pulling the hem down, even past her palms. *Turtling* some shrinks called it. A protective measure. Putting up walls, or physically manifesting a defensive posture. There were all sorts of terms and jargon to explain the same phenomenon. When Ilse stepped foot near danger or devilry, she often felt the return of childhood instincts.

She brushed her hair uncomfortably past her ear, feeling the eyes of the two police officers on her as they neared the trailer.

Sawyer, on the other hand, didn't seem at all perturbed by the audience. “Hey boys,” he said with a wave. “FBI.”

The two cops looked hesitantly at the agents. Ilse didn't blame them. This had been a problem for the two of them in the past as well.

Sawyer, lanky, wearing a baseball cap, dusty jeans from his woodworking, and a flannel shirt, looked more like a skinny farmer than an agent. And Ilse in her sweater, slacks and make-up free features looked like a stay-at-home mother rather than an investigator.

Sawyer often didn't go for his ID, preferring that cops just take his word for it. Ilse, more accustomed to the way people interpreted unspoken signals already had her ID in hand, holding it up.

The two cops blinked in surprise and shared a look. One of the men, in a neat, silver chinstrap and prematurely wrinkled eyes, glanced between them both. “Need anything from us, or we good to take a cigarette break?”

“Take it,” Sawyer said. “Grab some snacks while you're at it.” He waved into the studio. “Don't look like anyone else is gonna anytime soon.”

The cops both looked grateful all of a sudden and nodded in appreciation as they stepped away from their posts and began moving towards the open, studio door. The older man's hand slipped into his pocket and pulled out a pack, his other hand reaching for a metal lighter dangling at his belt.

Sawyer pushed open the door to the trailer, and immediately Ilse detected a sudden, pungent odor of cleaning liquids.

Sawyer began to step into the trailer, but then suddenly stiffened. Ilse froze, heart leaping.

Sawyer paused a moment, but seamlessly took what he saw in stride. “Who are you?” he said, his tone calm.

Ilse stared, wide-eyed, as a young woman in a white lab coat raised her hands skyward, her own eyes the size of saucers as she stared at the two agents in the door.

“I—I—who—forensics!” she stammered hastily, shaking her head hurriedly. “Sorry, sorry—didn't mean... didn't know... just—just was told to finish up!” The young woman was somewhat round with a pretty face. She glanced past Sawyer and Ilse, suddenly frowning towards the two cops who were both snickering as they moved towards the concessions table. "They didn't tell you I was in here?" she said, breathing heavily, and glancing warily at Sawyer's hand.

The lanky agent removed his fingers from his holster, grunting. "Nah. Didn't. Forensics who?"

"Umm, just—I work for Doctor Avery. Look, I'm just finishing up."

"What's your name?" Ilse asked, her rapidly pounding heart returning to a more appropriate rhythm.

"Oh, yeah, umm, Sonya," she said, quickly. The young woman shifted again, and Ilse spotted her gloved hands and a stack of plastic bags clutched in her other hand. There was a container that looked like a translucent toolbox at her foot, just within the door, as well as a row of swabs and miniature glass tubes resting on top of the box.

"Need us to come back later, Sonya?" Ilse asked.

The woman sighed, glancing back, but shaking her head. "Umm—no, no, that's fine. I can grab the last of what we need after. Most of it is already done. Blood is already cleaned," she added with a brightening tone as if hopeful this might please the two agents outside.

Sawyer just sighed, but to his credit kept his temper in check. Ilse nodded politely, waiting patiently for the younger woman to catch the non-verbal cues. When she didn't, Sawyer and Ilse both spoke simultaneously.

"Get out," Sawyer said.

"Could you please step out for a moment," Ilse said.

The woman's mouth widened. "Oh—oh, yes, sorry, so sorry. Just—yes. Here, look, let me put these here. All yours—it's all yours."

She placed the baggies on top of the translucent box, then stepped down to the pavement and slipped past Sawyer. The woman was quite short and couldn't have been a hair over five foot.

"Hang on," Sawyer said suddenly. "You got ID?"

The woman's eyebrows went up. But her hand darted into her white coat and hastily pulled out a lanyard which she presented to Tom. After a quick examination of the badge, Sawyer looked her in the eyes, which forced him to tilt his gaze down, and he said, "What are you still looking for?"

"Oh, the usual," the young woman said quickly. "Blood. Semen. Prints. All of it."

"Find any?"

"Lots of blood, but from the victim."

"Any semen?" Sawyer said not batting an eyelid.

"N—no. Not yet. I'm hopeful though," she said, brightening. "I'm good at this, actually. Very good. Dr. Avery doesn't normally hire people without much field experience. But... well, you know, not to brag, but I tend to find things others don't." She beamed at this, nodding. "I was the one who found the chipped tooth of the ice-truck killer."

Sawyer suddenly looked impressed. "Really? That was you?"

She grinned now, a cheeky, mischievous smile. "Yup, yup."

Sawyer scratched his chin. "It true you found the fragment in the victim's own mouth?"

"Yeah! I wouldn't have looked either, but there was something about the way the lips were that didn't match with rigor mortis post coitus... anyway...," the woman shrugged.

"How old are you?" Ilse said, frowning.

Sonya blinked. "Oh. Umm. Twenty," she said. "Well, I will be next month."

"You're nineteen?" Ilse asked, gaping.

Sonya flashed an uncertain smile. "Finished school in two years when I was sixteen. Still in grad-school. But Dr. Avery doesn't mind."

Ilse stared in wonder. Sawyer looked less impressed and was glancing into the trailer now. "What can you tell me that I don't already know?" he asked, waving a hand into the crime scene.

The young woman suddenly straightened. Some of her nervous energy depleting to be replaced by an eager tone. "The victim," she said without missing a beat, "was nude when attacked. Not after. No sign of discarded or missing clothing. I already checked with wardrobe on set. She was stabbed in the lung first. And from there was tortured." Sonya's expression didn't change at all as if she were reciting a school paper rather than speaking of horrific things. "Superficial cuts mostly, to the face. Those *weren't* what killed her."

Ilse blinked. "That's not what the report says."

Sonya winced. "I'm sure Dr. Avery will alter it once he gets a chance for a thorough examination."

"You disagree with the coroner?" Sawyer countered.

Sonya hesitated, shifting nervously on one foot. "Ummm... No. Just... It was the cut across the throat that did it. She was still bleeding; you can see by the spray pattern that blood vessels were still pumping. I found blood on the clothing rack—which would've been above the victim. Now, perhaps it was possible the killer kept waving around his weapon, but it doesn't seem so because the superficial cuts on her face were connected, meaning it required precision. The stab wounds *afterwards* were done once she'd already died."

"Let me get this straight," Sawyer said frowning. "You say the killer stabbed her lung to incapacitate, tortured her, killed her, then stabbed her again to mutilate?"

"Yes," Sonya replied without missing a beat.

She was still holding her lanyard in one hand as if uncertain what to do with it now. Ilse glanced at the ID again and noticed the last name. *Sonya Avery.* A relation to Dr. Avery, the coroner, perhaps?

Sawyer glanced into the trailer, and Ilse followed his gaze. A clothing rack set next to an open window and a floor-to ceiling mirror. Small little lightbulbs framed the mirror, but they were dead.

Sawyer nodded towards Sonya Avery, then slipped past her, stepping into the trailer. Ilse followed, murmuring, "Thank you," as she passed. The young woman, the teenager, just nodded quickly, taking an exaggerated step back as if to prove she didn't want to be underfoot at all.

Ilse smiled in what she hoped was a reassuring way. She paused on the steps of the trailer, studied the younger woman, then murmured. "Don't let them get to you," she said, glancing past Sonya towards the two cops by the concessions table. "You're doing good work."

The young woman beamed, her cheeks reddening. Then, Ilse nodded once more as if to seal her words and stepped into the trailer as well.

Sawyer frowned as he scanned the space. Most of the blood had already been cleaned, and the strong scent of cleaning fluids filled the air.

Sawyer glanced towards the window, which was ajar, then back at the mirror. "He came through there," Sawyer said, pointing.

Ilse approached the window, glancing out of it. The second trailer created a small alley against the studio's street-facing wall.

"Anyone might have seen him," Ilse said. "He just climbed through a window?"

"No one saw him," Sawyer replied. "Cops on duty questioned everyone on set. No one saw anything."

"They must have *heard* something," Ilse countered.

Sawyer just shook his head, staring through the ajar window, then glancing back towards the mirror.

"She would've," he replied with a grunt. "She definitely would've."

Ilse shifted uncomfortably at the thought. “He wanted her to see him coming,” she said. “That would fit with a sadist. They feed on fear.”

“The torture does too,” Sawyer replied. “That marathon runner—his legs were stabbed.”

Ilse glanced towards the mirror now as well, studying her own reflection. “Think that's relevant?” she murmured.

“Yup. Think so. Figure why?”

Ilse hesitated, but then winced. “A runner—so he stabs the legs. A model, so he cuts the face. He's taking what is valuable to them. He's making a statement.”

“Pride,” Sawyer said simply. “Grisly pride.”

Ilse looked back towards the thin man. “Why do you say pride?”

“He thinks he's smarter than us,” Sawyer said with a shrug. “Broad daylight—hunts 'em, kills 'em, gets away with it. Did it again. This is hubris.”

Ilse bit her lip. “If it's pride, something must have triggered recently, yes? Prideful people don't normally torture strangers to death.”

“We don't know they were strangers.”

“Perhaps not.”

“Maybe that's how he got them alone,” Sawyer returned. “Maybe they knew him.”

Ilse paused, considering this. “I—I don't know. Why climb through a window, then? Besides, knowing his victims—I don't think it would've mattered to a sadist with anger issues motivated by a sense of superiority.”

Sawyer snorted. “You saying Rawley did it?”

Ilse rolled her eyes. “Be serious.”

“I am,” Sawyer muttered, his eyes twinkling. “But we should figure out if our killer knew the victims.”

Ilse hesitated, but then nodded. “Adelaide Stevens was local,” she said. “Her driver's license record has always been in Washington. Her family might know something.”

Sawyer tucked his tongue inside his cheek and closed his eyes for a moment as if bracing against a sudden chill.

“What is it?” she asked.

“Nothing,” he muttered. “Just don't like talking to grieving parents.”

Ilse winced. “Do you have a better idea?”

Sawyer released his pent-up breath. “Nah. You're right. Let's go.”

Ilse exited the trailer first, glancing towards where the cops and the young forensics assistant were standing near the concessions table. She remembered what it was like to be young, working on her degree, working with Dr. Mitchell, her mentor.

She'd come so far, it felt like.

Then other days, like when she received those postcards, it was as if she hadn't changed at all.

What a troubling thought.

She frowned to herself, moving back in the direction of their idle vehicle. Sawyer was right, of course. Speaking with grieving parents was hardly an enjoyable prospect.

But they had to start somewhere.

And sometimes, the only path to true answers was *through* the painful experiences, rather than around them.

CHAPTER SIX

The large, suburban double-lot outside Seattle carried a gloomy countenance beneath graying skies as they pulled into the cracked asphalt driveway. The blue-siding and darkened windows gave the home an almost lunar glow.

Ilse spotted, through the windshield, the two figures standing in the already open door. Mr. and Mrs. Stevens had agreed to meet with them on short notice.

"Looks like they're ready to get on with it," Ilse murmured beneath her breath.

Sawyer shot her a look and gave a quick nod. "Wouldn't you be?"

Ilse considered this and gave a faint shrug with a single shoulder. Together, the two of them exited the vehicle, and moved up the poorly maintained drive to the large house. The lawn itself was overgrown, and a portion of fence, leading into the back, was moldered.

The two figures in the doorway were similarly shabby, wearing old, worn clothing and sweatpants. Mr. Stevens had a long face with a sharp nose. Mrs. Stevens had curling hair a shade removed from auburn.

The two figures waited in the threshold, in the illuminated hall of their home as the two FBI agents moved up the drive, up the steps and towards the house.

"Hello!" Ilse called, raising a hand and twirling her fingers in a semi-wave.

The Stevens both watched her, not speaking as she drew near.

"Are you FBI?" Mr. Stevens asked at last as they reached the porch.

The wooden step creaked as Ilse moved off it and came to a halt next to Sawyer, facing the grieving parents of their second victim.

Mrs. Stevens had streaks of mascara along her cheeks. Beyond, in the direction of what looked like a kitchen, Ilse spotted a box of tissues sitting on a table.

"May we come in?" Ilse said.

The question went ignored. The two parents remained standing in the door. Mr. Steven said, "You mentioned on the phone it was urgent."

Sawyer crossed his arms, keeping his silence. He often did this when interviewing relatives, preferring to allow Ilse to do the talking.

While sometimes she appreciated this, other times she wished he would contribute something in the arena of commiseration.

"We're very sorry for intruding Mr. and Mrs. Stevens," she said, "I'm sure you know why we're here."

Mr. Stevens just watched her, his expression haggard. His wife reached up, wiping some of her streaked mascara over a wrinkled cheek.

"I suppose you two should come on in," Mr. Stevens said at last, taking a movement back and making a gap for the two agents to join them in the entry room.

Ilse nodded in appreciation. She and Sawyer followed Mr. Stevens down a hall, towards the previously noted kitchen table.

Mrs. Stevens remained behind to shut and lock the door. Ilse heard a faint sniffle and the sound of creaking footsteps against old floors as the wife made her way slowly after them.

An old-fashioned teapot sat on the gas stove, whining and shooting a jet of steam. Mr. Stevens ignored this, pushing a foot against the wooden leg of the nearest chair and indicating it with a grunt.

Ilse sat first. Sawyer preferred to stand, leaning against the fridge, and watching all of them like a hawk. Mrs. Stevens slipped past him and sat at the chair nearest the box of tissues. The trashcan behind her was already overflowing, more than one tissue crumpled on the ground. A sleek, black cat was sitting on the counter, having shredded one of the tissues with its claws. The cat stared at Ilse with its yellow eyes, and she returned the glare.

Cats, like people, often came in two sorts. She didn't like the way this one was eyeing her. The cat leapt from the counter, nimbly landing on the ground, and stalked forward, investigating the newcomers. Ilse tensed as it brushed against her legs where she now sat in the indicated wooden chair.

"Don't worry, he's friendly," said Mr. Stevens, noticing Ilse's discomfort. "I don't know what else we can tell you. We spoke to that officer last night for nearly three hours." He gave a shaky little sigh and massaged his head in his hands.

The teapot behind him continued to whistle.

Sawyer leaned over, turning the stove off. Neither of the homeowners seemed to notice.

"Tea?" Mrs. Stevens asked, glancing at both of them.

"Thank you, yes," Ilse replied. Sawyer just shook his head.

Mrs. Stevens nodded, sniffed, but then her eyes grew vacant, and she stared off at the fridge for a moment. When she refocused, it was as if she'd completely forgotten what she'd asked to begin with.

"Your daughter," Ilse said slowly, "Adelaide... She still lived with you?"

Mrs. Stevens sighed, nodding. "She was going to move in the next few months." She sniffed, her fingers nudging the tissue box. "To New York, of all places."

Mr. Stevens shook his head in disapproval. "Too far away. It's not a safe city for girls like Adelaide. But she simply won't listen to reason."

Ilse fidgeted uncomfortably, noting the present tense way in which the father spoke. She didn't point this out, though, but instead said, "So she was moving to New York? Did she have a job?"

"Her modeling agency," Mrs. Stevens said, sounding proud all of a sudden. Her eyes brightened somewhat. "She was really, really good, too. A lot of people wanted to work with her. The contracts were starting to pile up, you know. She bought me my new car... A green one," Mrs. Stevens said, her eyes brimming again. "I love the color green..."

Ilse averted her gaze out of respect, glancing towards the husband now. "I'm obviously very sorry for your loss. I can't begin to imagine. Is there anyone you know who might have wanted to harm your daughter?" Mrs. Stevens winced. Ilse quickly added, "I know it's a hard thing to consider, but we have to look at all angles."

Mr. Stevens just shook his head. "No one. Adelaide wouldn't have hurt a fly. People loved her. Especially now after... well...," he glanced uncertainly at his wife who'd gone still. "It just... just wasn't like it used to be," he finished with a helpless little shake of his head.

"What does that mean?" Sawyer interjected. "How did it use to be?"

In answer, Mrs. Stevens got to her feet, moved past the fridge towards a drawer. "She hated it when I hung the old pictures up. Wanted me to burn them, but I couldn't. I loved her just as much then as I do now... But life can be hard on little girls. Especially if... well... if they're not a certain way."

"Martha," Mr. Stevens admonished. "I'm sure the agents aren't interested in old family photos."

"Actually, sir," Ilse cut in, "anything you think is relevant we'd be happy to take a look at."

Mr. Stevens shrugged, settling back in his chair while Martha returned, holding a wooden frame. She set the photo on the table in front of Ilse. In it, there were three figures. The husband-and-wife couple looked the same as they did now, though perhaps with a few less gray hairs.

The girl in the picture, though, didn't look anything like Adelaide had in her more recent driver's license photo.

The fashion model had been beautiful, sculpted, with perfect features. The girl in the photo was... quite plain. Ilse tried not to look surprised, studying the photo. The young teenager had braces, acne, and carried twenty or so pounds extra. She had a big, hooked nose, like her father, and round, bulging cheeks that hinted at baby fat which should have melted years ago.

"You have a lovely family," Ilse murmured.

"Had," Mr. Stevens corrected. "She had her whole life ahead of her. We thought things were changing, improving for her... But... but...," he sobbed, shaking his head. "That's what you get for hoping, I suppose."

Martha patted her husband on the hand, nudging the tissues towards him. In a quavering voice, she said, "Growing up, Addy thought she was ugly—which wasn't true at all. Not at all. But she was a bit ungainly and... and kids can be so cruel." Martha closed her eyes, letting out a faint sigh. "I know I could have done more. I—I wanted to be a great mother. Wanted to give her everything I could. But... but I know I didn't. And now I can't take it back."

"Dear, you can't blame yourself."

Martha sighed. "I know. I don't. I... but if I'd just been a bit more encouraging. Maybe if I'd home-schooled her instead of sending her to that horrible, horrible place with all those bullies."

"How long ago was this?" Ilse asked.

"Ten years?"

Ilse nodded. "So she had surgery?"

"Yes... Multiple. She wanted to... to *fix* herself," Mr. Stevens scowled. "I hated when she said that. She didn't need fixing. She was my princess. But... parents can't protect their children from the world. You want to try, though. You always want to try...," he drifted off, closing his eyes as if against a sudden jolt.

"Surgeries like that," Ilse murmured, "they would have been expensive, no? Did she take out loans? Borrow money from anyone?"

"No, no, nothing like that," Martha insisted. "We were more than happy to help her. Our jobs allow us some of the nicer things in life... We thought... we hoped that if we helped her, she might grow a little more confident. Might see herself as we did. But now...," she trailed off again, her eyes once more filled with guilt.

Ilse again was filled with an urge to reach out and just hug the woman but decided this probably would be too grave a breach of protocol. Still, her heart went out to the grieving parents.

"How much?" Sawyer cut in, raising an eyebrow.

"Excuse me?" Mr. Stevens asked.

"How much did all the surgeries cost?"

"I... I don't have a number off the top of my head."

"Ballpark it."

"Is that really necessary?"

"Where there's money, there's often motive," Sawyer said with a shrug.

Mr. Stevens hesitated, frowning, but then muttered, "Tens of thousands. Don't know exactly how much."

Ilse blinked in surprise. Sawyer just nodded grimly.

"Anything else you can think of?" Sawyer asked now, pushing away from the fridge and standing behind Ilse's chair. "Anyone your daughter might recently have mentioned in conversation. Was there a boyfriend involved?"

"No boyfriend," Mr. Stevens said. "She was too focused on work for that."

"She still didn't think anyone would love her," Mrs. Stevens added, shaking her head sadly. "Even after all that work. It was horrible... We loved her before any surgery. I know someone would've seen the same things we did. But... but now..."

"She would hit the gym every day," Mr. Stevens added. "That stupid twenty-four-hour place—Jade Fitness. She'd practically live there, hours a day. I mean I guess it was worth it to her. She *was* a rising star in the fashion world..."

Until now, Ilse thought to herself. She kept her expression compassionate, meeting each of the parents' gazes when they spoke.

Sawyer cleared his throat. "One last question, then we'll get out of your hair."

All three figures looked towards him now, including Ilse. Her eyebrows twitched, threatening to rise but she quickly hid her surprise. Sawyer normally didn't like taking point in interviews. She'd never seen him talk so much to the bereaved.

"Do you guys know anyone by the name of Arthur Lehman?"

The parents looked puzzled. Martha began to shake her head, but her husband cut in. "Is that who did it? Is that the monster who killed our Addy!" he yelled.

"James, please!" Martha interjected, holding a hand against her husband's suddenly tensed fist.

Ilse quickly said, "No, no he isn't a suspect. He was...," she glanced at Sawyer who didn't react so she continued. "He was another victim."

"Another victim..." Mr. Stevens said, the energy rapidly depleting as he slumped in his chair. "Jesus. No—no we don't know that name."

Sawyer flashed his phone, displaying a picture of the second victim. "Recognize him?"

But both Martha and James shook their heads, each adopting a thousand-yard stare as if looking through the phone.

Sawyer held it a moment longer as if to make sure, but then he withdrew the device, stowing it back in his pocket. "Well," he said, "If there's anything you can think to add, I can be reached by the number I called you on. Anything at all."

The parents didn't look much liked they'd heard.

Ilse felt Sawyer tap her shoulder and she got slowly to her feet. "I'm very sorry," she said again, swallowing. Part of her wanted to blurt out more. To make promises that it would all be okay, if they would just remain strong, together. To tell of all the testimonies of her clients who had recovered from similar situations.

But another part of her knew it was too soon for any of that. Pain had a funny way of drowning out hope. Even the realistic type.

She could only wish that when the time was right, someone would come along who could help the Stevens family to recover, to rebuild. But they'd lost their only child, their daughter. For now, all that lay in store was pain and each other.

She sighed, murmuring a quiet farewell which fell on deaf ears and turning to follow Sawyer back up the gloomy hallway, towards the front door. Sawyer unlocked and unbolted the door and stepped out onto the porch as Ilse followed.

The cool wind beneath the gray skies picked up, ruffling Isle's hair and chilling her exposed skin. The door shut behind them. Ilse heard the sound of footsteps on old wood, then the locking and bolting of the front door. She shivered, rubbing her hands along her sweater sleeves.

"What now?" she murmured, standing on the porch, facing the street and glancing up at her lanky partner.

Tom hesitated, adjusting the brim of his cap. Then said, "Victim one, I guess..."

"Does he have family in the area, too?"

Sawyer shook his head, but then began taking the steps towards the street.

Ilse frowned, following. "So how are we going to check his background?"

"Don't need relatives," Sawyer said. "I've got Rudiger." He glanced at his watch. "It's almost noon. Hopefully that means Rudy has woken up already. It's honestly fifty-fifty."

Ilse blinked remembering previous interactions with the flamboyant, Hawaiian-shirt wearing, jellybean eating FBI tech. He would make off-color jokes and seemed to live to see Sawyer blush, but he was also a whiz with computers.

"Think he'll be able to find a connection between our victims?" Ilse murmured, glancing back towards the gloomy house as they reached the street and moved towards their parked car.

Sawyer shrugged. "If anyone can, it's Rudy. Here, you drive. I'll call. He can get grumpy if someone wakes him up."

CHAPTER SEVEN

Tom rested his feet on the dash as Ilse drove them back through the city to the other side of town in the direction of HQ. She wasn't talking now, but watched the road with a keen, attentive eye. He valued that about her—she wasn't a chatterbox like some women he knew. His ex-wife, for instance. Then again... most men talked too much too. The whole damn species had a motor-mouth problem.

Not the least of which belonged to the man on the other side of the connected line.

"Damn it, Tommy," Rudiger's far-too-dramatic voice called into the phone. "It's the crack of dawn, you hoodlum!"

"It's almost noon, Rudy," Sawyer replied, his eyes hooded. He leaned back, relaxed. Despite the name calling and the feigned offense, he knew Rudiger wasn't really angry. He wasn't sure the big techie even had the ability to get *truly* mad. He was a sweetheart at his core, not that Sawyer would ever be caught saying it out loud. Rudiger would never let him hear the end of it.

"Noon? Noon! It's midnight in China, Tommy!"

"You in China?"

"That's not the point."

"Look, I need some help on something."

A pause.

"Is it about that cute little FBI agent you like?"

Sawyer had put the phone on speaker, and out of the corner of his eye he thought he caught Ilse smirking, but she hid the expression.

"You're in dreamland, Rudy," Sawyer said, putting a bit of a growl to his voice. This time, he looked straight ahead, not glancing towards Ilse. "It's about a case."

"Ah, shit. She's there with you, isn't she? I take it all back, my dear! Sawyer is no Prince Charming; I'll tell you that. He bludgeons your beauty sleep if you're not careful!"

"Hi Rudiger!" Ilse called, leaning in, and definitely smiling now.

"Ah, she is there—what a melodious voice, my dear. I hope Sawyer isn't causing you too much of a headache."

Ilse hid her smirk, though her eyes twinkled. "We need help on a case, Rudy. We're looking to connect two victims."

"Alright, alright," he said with a long, exaggerated sigh. "I'm only on call for my use, I see. Oh well, give me a moment."

Sawyer waited, listening to the sound of heavy breathing and panting from the faint motion, no doubt, of Rudy moving from his bed to his computer room. As the tech lived in a mobile home, the journey couldn't have been more than a few steps. But the big man wasn't exactly in the best of shape and so he panted for a moment longer, gathering himself before Sawyer heard the clack of a keyboard.

"Two names?" Rudiger said. "Looking for a connection, yes?"

"Yeah," Sawyer said. "Want the names?"

"Psh. What do you take me for, an amateur? It's Adelaide Stevens and Arthur Lehman, yes?"

Sawyer blinked.

"Don't sound so surprised," Rudiger said. "I can practically see that dumb look on your face, Tommy. It isn't fitting for such handsome features."

"Rudy, get on with it."

"Of course, of course. You never could take a compliment. But it's the only serial case currently pending at your office, see? Logic. What a gift. But ah... let's go... hmm... no..." More clacking keys.

"They live near each other," Sawyer said.

"I see that... But not *that* near. Cities, like you, Tommy, are somewhat dense. We have nearly a half a million people in the radius where the two bodies were found."

"So... anything else? Parents didn't recognize the name."

"I'm checking their phones... but—no—no shared numbers. No shared friends. Didn't know each other at least that way. They lived on opposite sides of town."

"Our second victim was moving to New York soon. What about Mr. Lehman?"

"No dice. He has a driver's license from '06 in California. He's West Coast born and bred. Doesn't look like he's moving anywhere anytime soon, either... Well... never, actually. But you know what I mean."

"Credit cards?" Sawyer pressed.

"Was already in the middle of it—looking at food and restaurants now. But... hmm—looks like the two of them visited the same bagel spot... But, there's a five year gap."

Sawyer huffed in frustration. "Anything? There's gotta be a connection, Rudy. You're the best, right?"

"Don't you forget it."

"Prove it. Again. Find me a connection."

More furious keystrokes. At that moment, though, Ilse cleared her throat. Sawyer frowned, glancing over at her. He met her gaze as she drove on the open highway, circling the city from West to East. In the distance, he spotted the space needle against the gray horizon.

But as he studied Ilse's gaze, not so dissimilar in color to the skies beyond, like a storm on the verge of rolling in, he felt a sudden jolt in his stomach.

He shifted uncomfortably, not quite looking in her direction now. Thankfully, she also returned her attention to the road.

He was doing his best to play it cool, but it was uncomfortable being around Ilse... After he'd told her.

Even at the thought, a sudden cringing jolt shot through him. He tensed, his hand tightening on the phone and momentarily muffling the speaker. This was a happy accident, as Rudiger was now humming some old sea shanty which involved more than one thinly veiled reference to whores and booty.

But even Rudiger's ever cheerful personality wasn't enough to assuage Sawyer's discomfort. Now, it was his turn to shoot a sidelong glance in Ilse's direction. He didn't speak about his sister.

He never spoke about his sister.

Once, Agent Rawley had *tried* to get Sawyer to open up. When Sawyer had refused, Rawley had tried to play hardball by forcing him to see a shrink before issuing clearance. When Sawyer had confronted him, Rawley had said he was doing it for Sawyer's own good. Then... then Rawley had mentioned *her name.* Rebekah.

Sawyer wasn't sure what had happened next. He'd lost time. He'd seen red. When he'd come to his senses, he'd been standing over Rawley, his fist aching, his supervisor clutching a bruised cheek and shouting for security.

He'd been banished to the mountains for months after that stunt.

But at least Rawley had learned his lesson. After the disciplinary suspension and exile, the psych hold had been removed and he'd been allowed to continue investigating. Credit where credit was due—Rawley hadn't used the incident to ruin Sawyer like so many might have done.

But now... now he'd mentioned it.

To a damn shrink, no less.

He winced, refusing to look in Ilse's direction. Rudiger was saying something, but Sawyer didn't even hear it now. He just grunted noncommittally, staring out the window.

He could tell Ilse wanted to talk about it. He'd known she would want to. Perhaps that was why he'd told her—though he'd never much considered himself the cry-for-help sort.

No. Sawyer was more direct with his problem solving. He believed in going straight to the source. Currently, that source was serving three life sentences in maximum security.

But Sawyer was already working on an angle. He had friends who worked in corrections.

One way or another, eventually, once he figured out the path, he'd get his revenge. He'd been planning it for nearly five years now... But he didn't just want the guy shivved in a shower. He wanted the bastard to suffer. And to do that... he'd have to spring him from the prison.

Sawyer let out a faint little sigh, trying to push the thought aside as if fearful Ilse might somehow read his mind. She was uncanny with her ability to read people. It made him nervous sometimes. Having her on the team was a huge asset, but not if she ever sensed what he was planning to do with Rebekah's killer.

He shivered to think what might happen then.

She would try to stop him, no doubt.

And while he'd take a lot of shit from a lot of people, especially people he liked, in this one area, he refused to let *anyone* get between him and his revenge. Not even Dr. Beck.

He shivered at the strain of morbid thoughts, pushing aside the rising sense of animosity. It wasn't worth dwelling on such things. The last thing he ever wanted to do was hurt Ilse. But he would find a way around her if the time came.

It was ironic, really. Partnered with her.

The one person he'd met who literally dealt with the survivors of serial killers. She would want to talk about his feelings, to try and help him heal. Or whatever gobbledygook she got up to in her practice. But Sawyer wasn't interested in healing. He was interested in making a man suffer and then putting a bullet in his brain stem and painting the forest floor with the colors found only inside a grown man's veins.

Suddenly, Ilse cleared her throat and said, "Hang on, Rudy—can you look up memberships for health clubs?"

Sawyer blinked, forcing himself to refocus. The voice, which was muffled now, chirped from his phone. "What was that, sweetie-pie?"

"Rudiger, manners," Sawyer snapped. He raised the phone, so the speaker wasn't blocked.

"Sorry, honey-boo," Rudy said, his tone laden with mischievousness. "Health clubs, you said? That isn't a subtle hint, is it? I'll have you know, I'm quite happy with—"

"No, Rudy," Ilse protested. "I'm talking about our second victim. Adelaide Stevens. Her father said she spent hours at a gym called Jade Fitness."

Sawyer's eyebrows suddenly shot up. "Holy shit," he muttered. "You're right. Our first victim was a marathon runner."

"Exactly," Ilse murmured.

They waited, both of them staring at the phone held in Sawyer's hand. Ilse cursed, veering sharply to avoid a merging sedan and returning her eyes to the road, but her attention was clearly split.

Finally, Rudiger called out. "Jade Fitness? I got two of them. Looks like they're expanding—good for them. The American dream and all that."

"Hey! Focus!"

"Tommy, chill. I've got you, fam. Right here... Mhmm—back two years ago Mr. Lehman also had a membership to... you guessed it... Jade Fitness."

"Two years ago?" Sawyer asked.

"Do I sound smug? I don't mean to sound smug. Wait—no, yes I do. Adelaide Stevens has been there for *four* years. That's two years of overlap. Though math was never my strong suit. Now, give a kiss to daddy, Tommy."

"Thanks Rudy," Sawyer grunted. Then he hung up.

Ilse's hands had clearly tensed on the steering wheel as they tore through the city streets. "What are the odds?" she asked quietly.

"Of both attending an obscure gym?" Sawyer replied, feeling the same weightiness all of a sudden. "Low," he muttered. "Gotta be low. It's not much, though."

"No, but it's a connection. The only one we have."

Agent Sawyer glanced at Ilse. If he didn't know better, he might have thought she was starting to get excited by the whole thing. He hid his own smile, nodding slowly to himself and cycling through his phone again for the GPS.

It took a moment, but then he said. "I got an address. Hang on. Take the next exit on the right. The gym is only ten minutes from here."

CHAPTER EIGHT

When they lied, it made him angry. But there were other things that angered him as well. Many other things. And now, he scowled across the field, watching the man on the old, green tractor chug gamely along, circling once, reaching the end of his field, turning, and circling back.

Such a predictable pattern.

The man with the black gloves glanced over his shoulder, towards where he'd parked his own vehicle on the side of the dirt road. He hadn't tried to hide his car. He found this sort of behavior only attracted *more* attention.

Now, he stood on the tilled dirt, facing the old tractor and the farmer riding it.

Beneath the sunlight above, peeking through the dark, gray clouds, he felt warmth against his skin. A car zipped by behind him, and he waved cheerfully at it. The occupant in the front seat looked bemused but waved back—a very similar reaction to the hospitality of the Amish.

Not that he was Amish. He wasn't much of anything... except he considered himself a storyteller. A master of happy endings.

The tractor turned, faint plumes of smoke rising from the exhaust as the vehicle moved once more down the rows of old weeds and over-long grass, cutting everything in its path.

Now, the man moved onto the farmer's ground, ignoring the tilled earth, ignoring the cleared field, ignoring, even, the lingering scent of fumes on the air.

He walked forward, smiling as he did, congenially, shoving his gloved hands into his pockets. As he drew nearer, leaving footprints behind in the mud, the farmer looked suddenly up and over. The man's face, beneath his straw hat, broke into a frown. He gave the approaching man a severe look, but this didn't deter him. He kept approaching the tractor and its rider.

At last, the farmer leaned down, turning off the engine, and coming to a sudden halt. He waved at his sweaty face with his large hat, then glared towards the approaching pedestrian.

"This is private property, sir," the farmer said with a snap. "You shouldn't be here."

The man with the black gloves kept his hands in his pockets, smiling up at the farmer on the tractor. "I know," he said cheerfully. "Nice place."

The farmer blinked. "Right... nice. Mister, you better get off. This is my land."

"I know. You're Jackson, right?"

Lee Jackson, the farmer, blinked. "Do I know you?"

"Not yet," the man with the gloves said, rocking on his heels and leaving impressions of his shoes in the dirt. He'd have to clear those later. But for now, he just enjoyed the chat. He liked chatting with them before it happened. Especially in broad daylight. It was his own little cherry on top, the frosting that made the cake so, so delicious. He'd tried to talk to that bitch back in the trailer, but she'd brushed him off. Then, in the trailer, she'd promised not to make a noise but gone and ruined that also. She'd screamed. She'd *lied.* So now, he was determined to enjoy himself.

"Well, then if I don't know you, and you know this is my land, get the hell off." The farmer's eyes narrowed now.

But the man didn't move, preferring to stay exactly where he'd landed. Another car zipped by behind them, kicking up a cloud of dust. He'd parked his own vehicle in such a way as to obscure his rear license plate. All of it where anyone who cared to look would notice.

But no one looked. Ever. Not until after.

"Hey man," the farmer said, reaching slowly towards a glove compartment on the tractor. "Get lost. Now! I'm warning you."

"Oh? Warning? Lee, that's not nice. You have, what is it, a hundred acres here? That farm up the hill is yours, too. The little house with your wife and two kids? Super nice place if you ask me."

"Alright, mister, I warned you. Put your damn hands in the air!"

The man in the gloves stared at the handgun now waving towards his face. He didn't blink, didn't retreat. Just continued smiling, rocking on his heels, feeling the way the mud parted beneath his shoes.

"Nah, I won't," he said cheerfully.

"I'm calling the cops!" the farmer screamed.

"Nope, you won't," he said. "I'll leave."

"Yeah, you better!"

The man continued studying the farmer. This land, this place was the fellow's very own happily ever after. "You want to know how I know you won't call the cops?" he murmured faintly.

The farmer hesitated, frowning.

"Because," the man said, "you don't like cops, do you? Not after that incident in the seventies, hmm? Moving here from Ohio—thought you'd outpace it. But nah—not how that stuff works, is it, Mr. Jackson?"

Now, the fellow on the tractor's eyes bugged. His gun, still pointing, trembled in his hand.

The man smirked. "Lee Jackson. Two counts of assault. Sexual battery. Nice way to start over up here. Must have a very forgiving wife. I wonder if your kids know."

Lee Jackson just stared like he'd seen a ghost, or at least had been brushed by one. "Wh—what do you want?"

The man tilted his head slowly, studying the gun. "I wasn't sure at first. But then you pointed that at me. You don't deserve a happy ending, do you? No, no, you don't. Cheaters I've dealt with already. Liars too. But violent men? I deal with your kind sometimes also."

"What the hell are you on about. Get your damn ass off my land before I put a bullet in it! I mean it, now!" The farmer leaned forward threateningly, the sweat dripping down his forehead, along his upper lip.

The man in the gloves nodded once. Mr. Jackson had reached his limit. He could tell. Everyone, every human, had a limit. And he'd pushed up to that very boundary. So now, he turned, and as casually as ever, began strolling away beneath the gray skies streaked with sun.

"Hey! Hey! Who are you? Don't just turn your back! What's your name!"

The man began whistling as he strolled away.

He heard a sudden blast—a gunshot. The dust exploded off to his left. He paused long enough to glance at the muddy terrain, to smirk.

Then he turned back, twisting at the hips like some curving snake, and looked Mr. Jackson right in the eyes. Dead eyes met ones filled with panic. The eyes of a snake fixing on those of a frightened coyote. One of them a venomous thing, the other just a scavenger.

"I don't normally tell...," the man said. "But for you, for that…," he waved a hand towards the dusty ground. "I'll give you one chance." He turned fully, chest rising proudly, arms spread as if attempting to embrace the horizon. "Put a bullet in me," he said suddenly. "Do it now while you've got your chance."

Mr. Jackson's eyes bugged, staring in horror.

"No?" the man asked, quirking an eyebrow. "Come on. Do it. Go on..." The gun in the farmer's hand just trembled. The warning shot had been a bluff, of course. The man knew his targets. Knew the sorts that deserved the lives they had. Knew the sorts that were too cowardly.

The man pointed a gloved finger at the farmer on the tractor. "You're going to regret not killing me. Have a good day," he added, cheerfully, and then spun again and walked, even more slowly than before, back towards his waiting car.

No gunshots now. No shouting. Just a single spectator. Another car zipped by, kicking up dust.

The man, though, grinned as he slipped into his vehicle. He waved once more over the roof of his vehicle, then closed the door. The farmer was just staring at him, beginning to move the tractor to eye the license plate, no doubt.

But he was too late.

The man hit the gas, kicking up a cloud of dust before veering onto the road, and making good his getaway.

For now.

He'd come back later. He liked them scared. Liked their fear.

As he drove down the dusty road, glancing in his rearview mirror to witness the outline of the man still sitting on his slowly moving tractor, he felt a faint shiver of delight.

One hand on the steering wheel, partly watching the long road, his other hand moved towards the glove compartment. He opened it, glancing inside at his own special device.

A dark, plastic handle gripped a carbon-steel blade. A long, wicked blade, serrated on the back. The sort of knife made for gutting and twisting innards.

He lifted the knife, hefting it and straightening in his seat.

Then, whistling again, he began spinning the open blade between his fingers, enjoying the familiar weight against his knuckles, the scrape against his skin.

Oh yes... That farmer was going to regret not taking the shot.

CHAPTER NINE

Ilse frowned at the small, painted sign in the window of the flat, single-story gym occupying most of the center strip mall.

The windows were clean, but the sign was practically hidden. Jade Fitness clearly wasn't interested in advertising.

And yet, as they pulled to a halt, parked, and Ilse stepped out into the parking lot, she glimpsed many gym-goers through the large windows, moving on fitness machines or using the workout benches in the back near the rows of mirrors. She could hear the faint whir of the nearest elliptical and treadmills even through the window.

Sawyer didn't seem to care about any of it—his eyes were down, his hat low as he moved towards the rotating doors of the gym.

Ilse fell into step as well, keeping quiet as she did. Sawyer had preferred to pass their time in the car in silence. Even more silence than was usual for the man.

Was he intentionally avoiding speaking with her? The thought upset her somewhat. But she also knew what it felt like to bare one's soul to another. He'd done that. He'd invited her into a dark portion of his most hidden life.

Now, Ilse wanted nothing more than to help him. His own sister had been killed by a serial killer. A sadist. Not too unlike the man they were currently hunting. She worked with survivors for a living. Was that why Sawyer had told her? Did he want her help... maybe he just didn't know how to ask.

But as she considered this, she frowned, wrinkling her nose, stepping from the asphalt to the curb and moving through the spinning doors. Sawyer was just a step ahead of her.

Tom didn't seem like the sort of man who'd ever willingly work with a shrink. Especially not a friend...

They were friends, weren't they?

More than friends?

Ilse felt her cheeks warm at even considering the thought. She felt grateful at the distraction as Sawyer cleared his throat near the reception counter, and said, "Manager."

The teenager behind the counter blinked once, began to speak, likely searching to recollect memorized words, but Sawyer cut the young man off.

"Manager," he repeated, a bit more firmly.

The teenager hesitated but seemed to see something in Sawyer's gaze and then winced, nodding and turning on his heel, skipping and half-jogging through a door behind the counter as he retreated.

Ilse leaned on the marble counter next to Sawyer. The faint scent of sweat, rubber, and cleaning liquids all mingled on the air in the familiar odor of gyms everywhere. The door had barely swung shut before a new figure emerged, frowning.

The woman looked like she spent a good amount of her time on the machines herself. She was trim, wearing a pink tank top that displayed more than the usual number of tattoos and musculature. Her frown seemed a permanent fixture as she mean-mugged the two FBI agents across the top of the sticky counter. She opened her mouth to speak, but Sawyer beat her to the punch.

"FBI," he said in a lazy drawl.

Instantly, the woman's expression changed, as if suddenly rebounding. She blinked, shooting a quick vengeful look back towards the assistant behind the glass door who winced. Then, she cleared her throat. "You got proof of that?"

Ilse flashed her ID. Sawyer didn't bother.

The woman crossed her impressively toned arms. "You're not looking for memberships, are you?" she said in a flimsy attempt at humor.

Ilse rewarded the try with a smile, but then said, "I'm afraid we're looking into previous clients of your establishment. Do you own the place?"

"Nah. Just manage. Who are you looking into?"

"We'd like you to provide all the information you have on Adelaide Stevens and Arthur Lehman," Ilse said without missing a beat. "Phone. Address. Emergency contacts. Dates of joining the gym. Anything."

"I—I'm not sure I can just give you that info. You know. Health concerns."

"You're not a hospital," Ilse replied with a frown. "This isn't a medical facility. Are you really going to make us get a warrant?"

"Will have to shut the place down," Sawyer added, nodding towards the gym-goers behind them. "And we're just getting into the busy part of the day."

The manager hesitated, but then sighed, turning her attention to the computer behind the curving marble desk. She clacked at the keyboard, and then frowned. "What'd you say the names were?"

"Adelaide Stevens," Ilse replied, enunciating clearly. "And Arthur Lehman."

"Alright, yeah. I got them both. They had the special plus memberships. Looks like... Though Lehman hasn't been with us for the last two years. His membership ended in August." She looked up with a shrug, studying the agents' faces to see if this information would be deemed useful.

Ilse said. "What does special plus, mean?"

"Access to the sauna, permanent lockers, and one on one training sessions with personal trainers," the manager rattled off with practice ease. "Why? You looking?"

Ilse had to credit the woman's industriousness. This was the second time now she'd tried to recruit the investigators. "What sort of personal trainers?" she asked.

"Umm... Ah, well... Actually...," now, the manager was stuttering, her cheeks reddening as she stared at something on the screen in front of her.

Ilse watched curiously, Sawyer, sensing the same thing, leaned in. "What was their trainer's name?" Sawyer asked. "Same guy?"

"Umm, yes, in fact. It was the same person. Actually, Ms. Stevens stopped seeing trainers last year. Mr. Lehman saw the trainer up until he left."

"What was the trainer's name?" Sawyer asked, eyes narrowed, looking engaged all of a sudden by the way he leaned in, studying the woman.

"Nolan Kent," she said with a noncommittal shrug. She glanced off to the side though and paused long enough so it didn't look like she swallowed right after speaking the name. But the tell-tale signs of nervousness were all there.

"This Mr. Kent," Ilse said carefully, "does he still work with you?"

"I—I'm afraid not. Mr. Kent is no longer employed at Jade Fitness due to a mutual parting of ways."

"What sorta mutual parting?" Sawyer asked.

The woman's expression was a bit more like a mask now, and she stared straight ahead as she answered. "I'm afraid I don't have that information in front of me."

"Nah, but you know it," Sawyer said. Then, he added, "Lying to a fed is a crime."

The manager caved, looking panicked. "No—no, look. Just, Mr. Kent was rumored to have engaged in inappropriate conduct towards his clients. There were accusations. He was fired last year."

"The same year Ms. Stevens stopped training with an individual trainer?" Sawyer said with a significant tilt of his brow.

"I—yes, I suppose so."

"And were either Lehman or Stevens among those who filed complaints?"

The woman's eyes darted towards the screen, then back up again. "What is this about?" she asked carefully. "Because I'll have you know, Jade Fitness can't be found liable for the actions of an individual. We took all the necessary precautions, and, I'll add, most the incidents of inappropriate behavior were *off* premises. In addition—"

"We're not here about that," Ilse cut in. "We just need to know if either of them filed a complaint against this guy."

The manager hesitated, swallowing once. She opened her mouth, but Sawyer cut in. "Remember what I said about lying to a fed."

She closed her mouth again, glancing at the computer, then sighed. "I'm afraid that I had to personally handle one of the complaints. When I found out, I immediately took it to ownership. But yes... Yes, Ms. Adelaide Stevens did file a complaint of sexual harassment against Mr. Kent."

She winced, shaking her head and giving a sort of defeated sigh as she leaned back on her heels and glanced between the agents. "Is that all?"

"You got an address for the guy?" Sawyer said.

The woman shrugged. "Not available to me."

"Whatever," Sawyer muttered. "We can figure that out ourselves. Mind giving a brief description of this Mr. Kent?"

***

Back in the car, moving slowly through traffic, Ilse watched where Sawyer tapped his fingers impatiently against the steering wheel. She glanced down at his phone, which he'd handed her. She swiped at the screen, frowned. Swiped again, rubbing her finger along the glass. "Dammit," she muttered.

"Swipe up, doc," Sawyer muttered, glancing out of the corner of his eye. "Gotta swipe up—one of these days, you're going to have to join the twenty-first century, you know that?"

“I hate these things,” Ilse muttered, trying to swipe up, but still failing to open the device.

Sawyer gave a closer look, then snorted, returning his attention to the slow-moving traffic. “You got it upside-down doc. Flip it.”

She did, swiped, and finally the screen opened. She scowled now at the device, refusing to give Sawyer the satisfaction of a comment. Instead, she scanned through the file Agent Sawyer had pulled up earlier, outside Jade Fitness.

“You really think he's couch surfing?”

Sawyer shrugged. “You're seeing what I'm seeing.”

Ilse studied the phone screen. According to the file, Mr. Kent had been evicted from his apartment the previous year, just around the same time he'd been fired from the fitness center, suggesting he hadn't been able to keep up rent.

Now, they were heading towards Mr. Kent's only surviving relative's home—his mother.

“Think she knows anything about all this?” Ilse asked.

“Guess we'll find out—here's our exit.”

Ilse gripped the armrest as Sawyer whipped the vehicle, a bit more rapidly than necessary in her assessment, onto the ramp, curling around towards the suburb where Mrs. Kent's home was located.

Sawyer followed the chirp of the GPS and turned down a side street, moving to the far end of a cul-de-sac set against a small, wooded area with a playground that was completely abandoned. As the afternoon stretched into evening, Ilse frowned in the direction of the numbers on the houses as they rolled by. Then, she clicked her fingers, pointing. “That one,” she said.

The home was a flat, single-story structure shaped like a shipping container with a roof.

A woman was sitting on the front porch, her legs curled up beneath her, a book in one hand and a glass of iced tea in the other.

As Sawyer pulled the car into the driveway, he muttered beneath his breath, “Don't see the son.”

Ilse frowned. “Think he isn't here?”

Sawyer hesitated, glancing ahead then frowned. “Truck in the driveway.”

“Your point.”

“Middle-aged women don't usually buy trucks. Less than eleven percent of truck owners are women.”

Ilse turned, staring at him. “How on earth do you know that?”

Sawyer just smirked, and pushed open his door, slipping out onto the asphalt and beginning to stroll towards the porch. As Ilse joined him, the two of them glanced up at the woman sitting there. She lowered her book slowly, frowning in their direction. The cover flashed, reading "Chicken Soup for the Soul."

The door to the house from the patio, Ilse noticed, was ajar.

Sawyer tapped his knuckles against the glass porch door.

"Hello," the woman said, nodding politely at each of them. "You selling something?"

"No ma'am," Sawyer replied. "FBI."

The woman shifted now, going still. She brushed a strand of silver hair behind an ear with the same hand she held the iced tea glass. The cold, condensed liquid streaked against her cheek. "I see," she said simply. "Are you here for my son?"

Ilse blinked at the direct nature of the question. Sawyer scratched the back of his head. "Yes, ma'am."

"He's not here."

Sawyer glanced towards the truck, then back at her. "Was he?"

She didn't hesitate but nodded. "He was."

"Recently?"

"About as recent as I can remember was the scrambled eggs that he had this morning at the breakfast table."

Sawyer crossed his arms. "Is that his truck in the drive?"

The woman snorted. "My boy—God bless his heart—ain't the truck driving sort. He's in one of those prissy electric things."

Ilse hid a smile as Sawyer cleared his throat. "Where is he now?"

The woman sighed, but didn't rise from her recliner, slowly picking her book up again but not quite reading it yet. "He's working."

"Working? We just came from his last filed place of employment. They said he hasn't been there for more than a year."

"He's freelance now," the woman said. "Leastways that's what he calls it."

"I see. And your boy, did he tell you why he was let go from his last job?"

The woman shook her head, the ice tinkling in her glass from the motion. "No, afraid not. Also afraid I don't quite wanna know. He's my son. He's welcome under my roof whenever he wants, but I'm damn sure not gonna lie to save him from his own choices. What'd he do this time?"

"We're not sure," Sawyer said.

Ilse glanced towards the man. She respected his decision not to mention the murders. No reason to upset the man's mother, even if—in fact—he was a sexual predator and a killer.

Ilse, though, had tensed as the conversation continued. If he really *was* the murderer, then the chances were he was still on the hunt. For all they knew, he would claim another victim before he returned—the killer was already moving at an extraordinary pace.

"So where's he freelancing?" Sawyer pressed.

"In-home training," the woman replied. "He's a personal trainer, you know." She sounded proud, but there was also a faint sadness in her eyes as they'd talked about her son.

Ilse's heart went out to the woman, at least, as much of her heart that hadn't already jolted in her chest at these previous words. In-home training could give him access to potential victims.

Sawyer seemed to have reached a similar conclusion. His tone went serious now as he said, "Any idea where he is now?"

She paused, lowered her book again, then sighed, rocking forward, grunting and rising to her feet. "I have the address in case of emergencies. You still didn't tell me what my boy did."

"Nothing nice," Sawyer replied. "Right now, though, we just want to talk to him."

"Right. That's how it starts. Talk." She shook her head, glancing towards the driveway, then back at Sawyer. She moved now towards the house, book in hand, pushing in through the front door.

"Excuse me," Sawyer called.

She just held up a finger as if to say *hold-on.* She entered the house, leaving the door open, and Ilse watched where she moved towards a corkboard against the wall. A second later, the woman snatched a piece of paper, pinned there, and returned, handing it towards the agents.

"There you are. That's the address he gave." She held onto it for a moment, meeting Sawyer's frown. "Just talk—that's what you said. Right?"

Sawyer made a crossing motion over his heart. "For the moment, yes. You have my word."

The weary mother still had that sad look in her eyes, but it was joined by a strange expression of inevitability. She just nodded, pushing the parchment forward. "He's a good kid," she said. "Or tries to be. He just... just lost his way somewhere." She shook her head, her silver curls shifting.

And Sawyer gently took the address from her hand.

But there was nothing gentle about his subsequent spin on his heel and hastened steps back towards the car.

"Thank you," Ilse said. But she was also moving, hurrying after Sawyer.

If Mr. Kent was their killer, they might already be too late.

CHAPTER TEN

Lee Jackson scowled from beside his barn, glancing in the direction of the house. He could see his wife moving about inside, her silhouette flashing across the glass. He glanced up at the darkening sky, wiping a hand across his sweaty forehead, dust spattering his fingers.

He'd spent the rest of the day near the house, within line of sight.

Ever since...

Since that odd occurrence by the west field. He frowned again, reaching for the grease rag on top of the tractor and stowing it back in the toolbox beneath the back wheels.

He could feel a strange prickle along his spine. People weren't normally so...*forward* as his unwanted visitor had been. Something had been off about the man. For one, he'd been wearing gloves, for another, he'd had a dead quality to his voice. Like a speaking cadaver. His eyes had been cold. Too cold.

He'd known men like that in prison before he'd been given his second chance. Before he'd started working the fields. Farming soybeans wasn't the most lucrative of jobs, but it paid the bills, kept him out of trouble and allowed the wife to keep an eye on him.

He kicked the toolbox, shoving it further under the tractor into the shadows, and then moved out of the barn, closing the large sliding door with a grunt, his muscles straining beneath his flannel.

Part of him had wanted to call the police, but the instant he did, they would look up his address, his record. Cops didn't treat people like Lee particularly nicely. No—perhaps his best bet was to avoid them entirely.

He had his own means of protection.

He brushed his fingers against his sidearm, feeling the cold, comfortable weight at his hip. The shotgun he'd left back at the house, but now with the pistol in its leather holster, he'd determined something else.

If that creep with the dead eyes and gloves ever showed up again, he'd bury the man beneath the soybeans. A man could only take so much. He'd served his time, hadn't he? But cops kept harassing him, the city kept forcing him to move. Notified his wife every year or so. It showed up on their tax forms, on his right to even legally *own* the firearm in his hand.

He was sick of it.

And now some hillbilly, some drifter, wanted to come on his land and threaten *him*? Nah. None of it. Not happening.

He wiped his hand, covered in equal parts grease and sweat, on the back of his already stained blue jeans and then began to move up the path in the direction of the large soybean silo behind the barn.

The last chore before the day was through. He had to check the humidity levels. Especially in a state like Washington, it was crucial to make sure the silo was still airtight. The last thing he needed was for all his hard work to go to waste by mold or mildew or rot.

He moved along the side of the large, gray barn, padding up the dirt path in his boots. He rolled his shoulders as he walked, wincing against a strained muscle. Then again, when weren't his muscles strained?

As he moved, he glanced towards the large, protruding storage tower. Vines crept up the side of the silo where it reached like a finger touching at the clouds. He frowned at the trailing dirt path, hesitating for one moment. The undergrowth had been cleared back from the edges of the road, but there were stray leaves scattered across the dust.

He frowned, kneeling for a moment, pressing his fingers against the grit. He looked up at the nearest tree, on the other side of the barn: a large oak, one of his wife's favorites. Why were there leaves here? He hadn't come this way since the morning, and the wind had been low through the afternoon.

A low chill arose in him.

He kicked and a few of the leaves scattered, his boot leaving a furrow in the ground to match the divot in his brow. He paused, glancing over his shoulder back up at the house. He frowned and glanced along the trail towards the bean silo.

No motion, no movement—nothing greeted him except the indifferent silence of night's reluctant arrival. The evening sky was darker now, it seemed. The bean silo larger, inflexible against the horizon. The sparse land surrounding the thing was open. No motion, no sign of movement at all.

"Come on, you ass," he muttered to himself. He was acting like a little girl. He twisted his lip into something approximating a sneer and began to stalk up the dirt road again, hand on his weapon, eyes attentive and wary.

As he neared the silo, the large thing appeared as a metal tube with a semi sphere cap. The wind was still, the horizon quiet. No main roads or highways came anywhere near his land. The silence was what some called deafening.

Now, in the dark, he frowned as he heard a faint *creaking* sound, coming from the storehouse.

"Hello?" he called, his voice hoarse.

No reply.

He reached for his weapon, pulling it slowly from his holster. He stared towards the silo.

"Anyone there?"

Again, no response. Faintly, he thought he detected the odor of cumin on the air. His wife had said she was making Kima for dinner.

Now, all he wanted was to turn on his heel, march back home, sit at the dinner table and forget all about creaking noises, empty, dusty roads, telltale leaves on dirt paths.

He wiped a hand across his brow and let out a slow, leaking breath.

The silo could wait until the morning, couldn't it? Yes... yes perhaps he'd call one of the boys from Little Mickey's to stop by and give him a hand. They were always willing.

On the other hand...

He stared towards the silo, a frown affixed to his features. But then, he let out a huffing breath and turned, a slow chill trembling up his spine.

Not tonight. He could check in the morning. Wasn't raining, wasn't particularly humid. The harvest would be fine for a night. He rubbed at the back of his neck, his pace quickening as he moved away, back up the path, along the side of the barn.

As he hastened away, he felt a faint sense of relief at the decision.

He wasn't scared of the dark. Not at all. But he wasn't an idiot either.

He passed the front of the barn, moving up the incline towards his home, but then went still. He frowned back towards the front of the gray structure.

The barn door was still open.

He hesitated, certain he'd slid the thing shut.

"Hey," he said, his voice severe. "Hey, who's in there? I'm warning you..."

Gun in hand, gun raised, he took a step forward.

His adrenaline was racing now, his heart pounding wildly. He angled his weapon towards the open door, his other hand now moving towards his pocket for his phone. Perhaps he ought to call someone...

just in case...

He pointed his weapon into the barn, frowning into the dark murk. The tractor was where he'd left it, the toolbox visible just beneath the back wheels. No sounds from within, no creak of old wood, no rustle of hay, no whisper of wind on the still night.

He scanned the barn, but then let out a faint huff of frustration, lowering his gun and gripping the handle of the sliding wooden door.

He grunted, trying to close it.

But it required both hands.

Another chill up his spine, but he sighed and holstered his weapon, summoning some inner courage and then gripped the handle with both hands. He began to jerk the door shut.

And that's when the ghoul emerged from the darkness.

A shape moving rapidly from just beneath the front of the tractor. A brief glimpse of a face streaked with grease and dust, hands clad in gloves.

He yelped, stumbling back on the dirt road, hand going to his weapon. But too late. Something plunged into his chest. A lung popped. His eyes bulged, and he tried to scream. Pain didn't come at first, but he sensed a numbness spreading across his pectoral.

He was on the ground. Strange. When had that happened?

The ghoul above him had his hand trapped, a knee pressed to his wrist. He couldn't reach his weapon. Could barely move.

"Mr. Jackson," a voice whispered in his ear, lips near his cheek. Hot breath pressed moisture to his skin. "I warned you... Pity."

Then another flash of pain. Another.

He tried to kick, tried to struggle.

But it was no use, he was trapped before his barn. The dull light from the farmhouse up the hill providing scant comfort as he bled out in the dirt.

CHAPTER ELEVEN

"Yeah—that one!" Ilse was saying, frowning from the paper note in her hand to the address on the side of the house. "No—no *that* one! Tom!"

Sawyer growled, "I see the Prius, doc. We're good!" He jerked the steering wheel along the side of the road of a neat, newly painted suburban house with no driveway. A water feature tastefully meandered through the neat grass garden. The home had no porch or patio but did boast an impressive oak door with a golden knocker shaped like a lion's head.

Ilse and Sawyer hastened to the front door, took a step onto the slab concrete platform, and both of them knocked simultaneously. And waited.

Ilse breathed heavily, brushing nervously at the hair over her maimed ear, staring at the sealed door. She glanced towards the Prius in the drive and felt a bout of nerves. "He's definitely here," she muttered.

"Yeah, alone... with a woman," Sawyer growled. He ducked his head, peering through one of the windows. "Dark upstairs," he said. "Shit. Hey!" he called, raising his voice. "Nolan Kent! Open the door! FBI!"

Ilse pressed the doorbell and a faint ding echoed from inside the home. But there was still no answer. Sawyer worried his lip, glancing sharply at Ilse. "Car's in the drive," he said, a faint glimmer in his eye as if trying to explain himself.

"I—yes, I see—what are you doing—!"

Ilse tried to protest, but Sawyer's elbow was in mid-motion. His flannel sleeve slammed through the glass of the nearest window. The oak door was too thick to try and kick down. But now, he scraped at the shards of glass with his sleeve, wincing as a faint trail of red crept down his elbow, soaking through a small rip in his sleeve.

Normally so calm, controlled, Sawyer looked... scared. Panicked. His eyes had a haunted, almost distant look to them.

Sawyer flung himself through the window, hitting the ground inside. Ilse stared, stunned, glancing over her shoulder and wondering if anyone was watching. Before she could ruminate though, the door clicked then swung in.

Sawyer stood in a dark entrance, gesturing urgently at her.

"Hear that?" he said. He blinked a few times and then looked at the scattered glass, frowning suddenly as if surprised. Ilse had seen PTSD before in survivors of trauma.

Ilse paused at the threshold, wondering if she ought to say anything, but Sawyer was already moving again. She swallowed her nerves and moved into the house. She paused long enough to frown and nod. She *did* hear that. Music—faint, strobing music.

"Coming that way," Sawyer said. "FBI!" he called again, louder.

But now, the music only seemed to increase as they padded down a hallway, away from the front entrance in the direction of a basement with a closed door.

Sawyer gripped the handle and yanked the door open.

The sound of music swelled up the stairwell, resounding in their ears and swishing through the hall. Ilse hesitated a moment at the top step, but then she heard the faint sound of grunting. The sound of a sudden *crash!* Then a scream.

"Shit," Ilse gasped, bug-eyed, her fingers scrambling for her weapon.

But Sawyer didn't take a second. He bound down the stairs like some sort of mountain cat, a snarl on his lips, but the sound restrained to conserve his breath. Ilse followed as quickly as she could, but Sawyer was moving so recklessly that he reached the bottom step, nearly striking into a wall by the time Ilse was midway down the stairs.

Once she was on the ground as well, she spotted a flash of motion as Sawyer lunged towards two figures in the middle of the room, near a couple of yoga mats. A big screen TV was flashing images, displaying people performing a workout routine. The music was so loud, Ilse's ears heart—the strobing, thumping rhythm and faint melody that was the cousin to elevator music everywhere.

Ilse spotted a ceramic pot—neat, new and well-kept like everything else in the house. It had smashed on the tiled ground in front of the TV, falling from the display cubby hole it evidently had resided in.

The two figures struggling on one of the yoga mats, though, soon snared her entire attention. A woman in a sports bra and workout pants was trying to scream, bucking her hips to attempt and dislodge a man who had her wrists pinned above her head.

His back was to them, the music completely overwhelming his senses.

The man had slick hair and muscles for days, which he boldly displayed in a short cut, two-sizes too small, t-shirt. He was panting, and saying, "Come on—you know you want to. Don't be a tease!" He began to say something else as the woman shifted and struggled trying to get free.

But the words never arrived, as Sawyer reached him now. Tom didn't pause, didn't shout, he just slammed right into the fellow, knocking him off the struggling woman.

The man's spine arched, and he let out a sound like a whoopie cushion followed by a *thud* as his meaty form hit the floor.

Sawyer landed on top, but then kept right on going, carried by his momentum. He rolled off the man. For a moment, Ilse just stared in horror. The muscular attacker groaned, but was slowly rising, shaking his head dully and muttering, "What the hell..."

The woman on the ground was scrambling to her feet, retreating back towards Ilse, eyes wide and in horror, searching for the first friendly face she could discover. "It's all okay," Ilse said quickly. "Holding out a hand. It's all—" then her eyes widened, her gun raised, and she pointed it towards the man Sawyer had tackled. "Drop it!" she yelled. "Drop it now!"

The jock had picked up a piece of the porcelain pot, holding it above his head. He heaved a breath, but then his small eyes fixed on Ilse, glanced to her gun.

"FBI!" she said. "Drop it, now!"

Sawyer, groggily, was rising to his own feet.

The man with the raised piece of pottery hesitated a second longer, his eyes suddenly registering what she'd said. "Aww, shit," he muttered.

Sawyer then clocked him from behind, catching him on the side of the head and sending him in a pile to the ground.

Gasping, wincing, his elbow bleeding, Sawyer stepped over Mr. Kent and looked towards the trembling woman who was staring in horror from her attacker to the gun in Ilse's hand.

"Are you okay?" Sawyer said, his tone earnest. "Miss, are you alright?"

She just stared, shocked, stunned. "A—are you really FBI?" she whispered.

"Yes," Ilse said. "You're safe. Don't worry. You're safe."

The woman bit her lip, inhaled shakily then let out a long breath.

Sawyer, once he seemed convinced the woman was alright, glanced back towards the man on the ground. He reached for his cuffs, muttering, “Under arrest...” before dropping to a knee and grabbing one of those muscular wrists.

***

Ilse crossed her arms where she sat across the table from Mr. Kent, frowning in his direction while watching him cry.

Sawyer's expression was impassive where he sat next to her. They were using the interrogation room of a local precinct which had only been a five-minute drive from the would-be victim's house. Ilse could still see the fear in the woman's eyes, and the sudden way it had changed to hope. Even still, an attack like this would leave scars. It would lead to long nights awake. Locked doors. Weapons beneath the mattress, phone calls to friends in fright. It would lead to reinforced windows, maybe even a move to another house.

Things like this traumatized their victims.

Now, though, Mr. Kent didn't look anything like the macho aggressor he had projected down in that basement. Alone, the sounds drowned by music, hidden from sight—or so he'd thought. A different animal had been released in the dark. A cowardly animal.

Across from them, someone else sat.

“I—I, I know I have a problem,” the muscle-bound personal trainer moaned, sobbing between breaths. “I know it... I—I shouldn't have done it.”

“Done what?” Sawyer said, his tone completely devoid of emotion, his eyes empty of anything near compassion nor condemnation. He simply watched the man, a puzzle to be figured out.

“A—attacked her,” he said between another round of sobs.

“You tried to sexually assault her,” Sawyer prompted.

The man just continued to sob.

“Say it,” Sawyer said. “You need to say it.”

The man just shook his head, his lips peeling back. “I—I didn't mean to,” he sobbed. “I swear it... I swear it, just, just... I'm sick. I know I'm sick.”

“Sick?” Sawyer said, some of his tone changing now, a layer of anger rising. “That's what you call it? *Sick*? That's one word for it. Scumbag is another. Evil is probably the clearest. So you do admit to it? You tried to rape her. Then what were you going to do, hmm?”

The man just shook his head, tears now streaming down his cheeks. He stared off, vacantly across the gray room, his shoulders trembling.

He didn't look like some big brutish jock anymore. Rather, he looked like a child. A large, bawling child with oily hair and a curled lip.

"I got twisted young," he was saying, sobbing. "Got twisted young... I didn't know—didn't mean to. Just sometimes, sometimes I can't help myself."

Sawyer grunted in disgust.

Ilse, though, remained quiet. She was thinking of the man's mother. She truly seemed to love her son, though she hadn't hidden him from them. Ilse could only imagine what her life might have been if she'd also had that sort of love. There was no father in the picture... Twisted young. What did that mean? Did it matter. This wasn't her client—she wasn't his therapist.

This man had chosen another path. He'd chosen to damage others for his own pleasure.

Part of Ilse pitied the man, but another part of her wanted to scream at him. She'd seen the cycle so often. Especially by those who came *late* to sessions with her. A cold, hard truth of her career: some of her clients, who'd survived, could cause damage to others. Oftentimes by putting up defensive walls to protect themselves, hiding from the world. But other times, they would cause more serious damage. She'd spoken to women and men before who had passed on the abuse, the fear of their altercations. She'd spoken to killers in prison, spoken to trauma-victims acting out in violence.

That was one side of the story. Hurt people hurt people. But on the other side, she'd looked into the eyes of children, of women—so often women—and seen them weep. Seen the scars that went deep. The majority of her clients only harmed themselves in response to their abuse or their traumatic events. They locked away, hid—they didn't deserve what had happened to them.

And so the cycle of victim and victimizer so often continued. People could use their pain as an excuse to damage others. And people could choose to help those who were in pain.

Sometimes, though, the only way to help a predator was behind bars.

Ilse thought of his would-be victim. Thought of the two other victims of the serial killer. No one deserved that. The whole world, sometimes, seemed as if it were in pain. Agony spreading like a virus. No one to do anything about it except to try and catch it before it was too late.

This was always the hardest part for her, when it came to the job with the FBI. She had two parts to her. Not just a law enforcement agent. Not just someone focused on the bad guys. She didn't think in such simple terms—not really. Good, bad... She looked at her own life, looked at her sister Heidi. Both of them brought up in the same home. If Dr. Mitchell hadn't found Ilse, hadn't acted like a second father figure... who knew what might have happened.

Heidi, on the other hand, had been abused just like all of the Muellers... things had turned out much different for Ilse's sister. Twisted young.

That's where it all started. Evil perpetuated itself. She didn't hate the man in front of her. She pitied him a bit. She felt rage at what he did to his victims. But also... she felt sad. Sad at it all. She wished she could just bleed all the pain, all the hurt out of the world.

Sawyer's tone didn't carry any form of pity, nor pain. He just looked mad. "And the first two," he said. "You rape them also? Is that it—you swing both ways, huh? The guys and the girls. Coroner didn't seem to think so but you tell me."

The man suddenly froze, staring at them. "The... wait, what? Coroner? What coroner?"

Sawyer snorted, pointing a finger that jutted out further even than his baseball cap brim. "We caught you in the act Kent. Don't play dumb. It will go way easier if you just own up to it."

Now, though, the man's eyes widened to the size of saucers, and he stammered horribly. "Own up to... I—I told you I had a problem. I didn't..."

"What? Didn't do this before?" Sawyer snorted. "Please. Nice try. We have a statement from the gym you used to work at. Complains of harassment. One from one of our victims no less. Is that where it started? Assault escalating to murder?" Sawyer shook his head, wagging that same extended finger. "It's always the same shit with you guys, isn't it?"

Now, though Mr. Kent looked as if he'd been hit by a truck. "Wait—what? I didn't—hold on. Murder? I wasn't going to—I didn't—I'd never!"

"Kill someone?" Sawyer snorted. "Right. What about your last two victims? They were clients of yours at Jade Fitness. One of them filed a complaint against you."

Now, the man's entire demeanor had changed. His face went from pasty and pale to straight-up horrified. He gaped like a landed trout, mouth opening and closing rapidly. "I didn't kill anyone," he said, all in one exhale. “I never! I got a little frisky, handsy maybe, with a couple of my clients at the gym. I'll admit it... But I never, ever hurt anyone!”

Sawyer seemed to spring up all of a sudden. One moment he'd been sitting, quiet and docile, the next he'd surged forward, eyes raging, neck muscles bugling. He slammed a hand against the table with a thundering *clap!* “Never hurt anyone? That's what you call what we walked in on?”

“That was an accident!” he moaned. “An accident!”

Ilse frowned, studying the man. He was lying to himself, that was clear. But was he also lying to them? Why admit part but hold back the rest? Feeding a grain of truth as a form of camouflage to deflect the rest?

Perhaps. Or perhaps he was telling the truth about the murders.

“Where were you this week?” Ilse said calmly, ignoring Sawyer's furious figure.

The man's eyes darted from Sawyer's glare to Ilse's stare. At least, with a swallow and a final nervous flick of his eyes to Tom, he settled his gaze on Ilse, pleading. “I was at my mother's after work.”

“So you had work?” Ilse said.

“Yes! Yes—I did!”

“When?” she pressed.

He now glanced at Sawyer again and back to Ilse, stammering, “All day—I work all day! It isn't cheap what I do!”

“You were working the afternoon on Wednesday?” Ilse asked.

“Umm... Umm, yeah that would've been the Kilo residence. Couple of old fellas. Nice folk.”

Sawyer looked frozen, like a marionette gone stiff. He glanced at Ilse, then back at the man across the table. He remained standing, but his clenched fest released after a moment. “You saying you had clients the last few days?”

“Every one of them!” the man exclaimed, wagging his head. “Yeah!”

“Got proof?”

“Yes. Yes!” The man's head wagged so wildly, his gelled bangs flapped up and down like one big fan. “I have my day planner in my phone. Any one of them can vouch for me. I'm good at my job—really... just sometimes... sometimes I get a bit overwhelmed and...”

“Christ,” Sawyer muttered. “I don't wanna hear your belly-aching. Pass-code for your phone.”

“Umm...”

“Pass-code!” Sawyer barked. “Now! You say you have an alibi?

Prove it. I'm going to call every one of those clients of yours. If you're lying...," Sawyer pointed a finger at the man, his eyes blazing. "You'll wish you hadn't."

"If... if I'm telling the truth," the man said in a hopeful, hurt voice, "does that mean I'm free to go?"

"Hell no," Sawyer snapped.

"No," Ilse said with equal firmness. "Sexual assault is a serious offense," she said. "You'll spend time in prison. But perhaps you'll be allowed out..."

"If you're telling the truth," Sawyer said. "Now give me the pass-code for your phone, dammit."

The man's head was hanging now and his lip jutting petulantly. But before he could start to reply, Sawyer's own phone began to ring. He growled in frustration, yanking the device out. He glanced at the screen, but before he could shut it off, he went still, staring.

Ilse watched Sawyer quizzically as the sandy-haired man lifted his phone and said in a hoarse voice. "Yeah?"

He paused. Ilse watched the way the muscles bunched around his eyes, feeling a rising sense of anxiety in her gut.

"You sure?" Sawyer said. He sighed, exhaling a breath. "Be right there," he muttered. He lowered the phone, staring at it for a second, then glancing to Ilse.

"What is it?" she murmured.

Sawyer's lips pressed in a narrow line.

"Another one?" Ilse said suddenly, eyes widening. "Another body, you're sure?"

Sawyer winced, glancing towards the man behind the table. He pointed a finger. "You stay put," he snapped. "I'll send a boy in blue in. Tell him your pass-code. Tell him everything you told us, hear me? Leave nothing the hell out!"

Kent just hung his head but nodded to show he'd heard.

Then, Sawyer looked back at Ilse, jerking his head to the door. "Let's go," he muttered.

"So it is?" Ilse said, trying to keep her words cryptic for the sake of their present company. "Another one?"

Sawyer rubbed his chin but closed his eyes and released a weary huff. "Yeah," he muttered. "Another one. Let's go."

CHAPTER TWELVE

Ilse shivered as she stared across the dusty road leading to the old gray barn. A large metal silo arose from the ground behind it. A farmhouse settled the top of a hill. Night had fallen now, and orange lights glared from the farmhouse towards the rest of the land around it. The last time she'd been on a farm with Agent Sawyer, they'd discovered a stack of bodies. Now, she could see the flashing lights of police cruisers up ahead where a new corpse had been discovered.

They had parked further up the path, where Sawyer had wanted to exit the vehicle and walk the rest of the way. As they moved, he frowned at the ground, studying the dust and the dirt, hands jammed in his pockets, lips drawn in a thin line.

Ilse moved slowly along behind the taller man, careful not to get in his way. Sawyer could get quite particular when like this. Also, she felt like she was getting to know him a bit more now. She'd seen the signs of PTSD back at the house, when smashing the window. For a brief moment, in his haunted gaze, Sawyer had transported himself somewhere else. He'd been running to save a woman in a basement... But the woman he'd been trying to save had been from a past life. She felt a surge of pity for Tom, but just as quickly refused to ever voice the emotion. He'd only resent her pity.

Plus, he was a damn good investigator. Like a hound searching for a scent, he scanned the road. After a few paces towards the barn, without even glancing towards the police gathered around the entrance, Sawyer took a step *off* the beaten path, into the undergrowth and rock-strewn, muddy ground lining the trail.

"See anything?" Ilse asked quietly.

Sawyer grunted once but kept going without reply.

Ilse let out a faint sigh, but kept her silence, allowing her partner to work in peace. After another few paces, Sawyer hesitated, then said. "Big silo."

She turned to look in the direction of the metal storage unit jutting into the air.

"What about it?"

Sawyer paused, taking his hat off and running a hand through his hair. “Farmer would've gone that way,” he said simply, pointing with his hat towards the silo.

“And?”

“Someone came this way.”

Ilse hesitated, leaning over the edge of the path and staring towards the indicated section of ground. “You're... sure?”

Sawyer clacked his teeth in an impatient sort of chomp and shrugged a bony shoulder. “Mhmm.”

Blue and red lights illuminated off the bean silo and the gray barn, casting long shadows and flitting shade across the roads. In the distance, thanks to the headlights of the cars, Ilse spotted the fields, flat, cultivated land as far as she could see.

“Is it true the farmer had a record?” she said.

Sawyer nodded once. He looked at her. “Sexual assault. He's on the registry.”

Ilse frowned. “Sexual assault? You don't think it has something to do with Kent, do you?”

Sawyer shrugged, pulling at his face. “Some men can be awful. Hate to say it, but it's more common than you'd think.”

“Predators,” Ilse said simply. “Not protectors.”

Sawyer stepped back onto the road, studying her, then shrugging once. “Guess not,” he said. “No. Not protectors.”

She noticed the way Sawyer scowled, moving up the road now in the direction of the cruisers and their flashing lights.

Sawyer paused, glancing towards the silo again, frowning now.

“Why do you keep doing that?” Ilse said, watching him.

“Hmm?”

“Looking off like that—what are you seeing?”

Sawyer glanced back at her. He massaged his jaw. “Missing vines.”

“What?”

“Vines—should be on the east side of that silo. Sun comes up over there, yeah? Vines are missing.” He pointed one way then the other, then lowered his hand. “Rest of the silo has vines. But that's a bald patch.”

Ilse frowned, looking in the direction where he'd indicated. Then she noticed it too. A damp, silver patch on the side of the silo amidst a forest of vines and green leaves.

“Huh,” she muttered. “Think that means something?”

Sawyer though had come to a halt, facing inside the barn now. Ilse's attention diverted, turning to look as well. As her gaze settled, flicking past an old tractor and a toolbox behind a wooden work bench, she went still.

Sawyer just looked into the barn, swallowed once, then said, “Yeah... yeah I think that means something.”

Ilse's eyes just bugged as she stared at the horrible spectacle inside the barn. She began to mutter beneath her breath, “BTK. Dennis. Ten. Wichita...,” but she trailed off as some of the officers inside the barn were shouting instructions at each other.

The man dangling from the rafters had been cut to pieces. Blood stained his naked chest, dripping down to his toes where it had congealed, thick and crimson. It wasn't rope that held him aloft, however, but a thick, green vine, with leaves attached. The vine wrapped around the man's wrists and neck and held him up, suspended in the air, dripping blood where it had pooled on the ground beneath him, spattering against the black tires of the tractor.

A couple of officers had climbed a wooden ladder to the loft and were trying to cut the victim down.

Ilse's lips felt numb as she stood next to Sawyer in the entrance of the barn.

“What was his name?” she murmured, her gaze fixated on the mangled mess.

“Lee Jackson, mid-fifties,” Sawyer replied, his voice grim. “A soybean farmer. Rudiger is still checking, but so far no connection to our other two victims.”

Ilse looked away from the body, wincing as she did. She didn't want to see it, but also couldn't unsee the image carved into the inside of her eyelids. “A soybean farmer?” she asked.

Sawyer grunted in the affirmative.

“It doesn't make any sense,” she whispered. “None of them are connected. Why is he choosing them? Is it all random?”

Sawyer hesitated, then muttered, “It's never random,” before striding forward into the barn to help lower the body from the loft.

CHAPTER THIRTEEN

Ilse could still see the image of the tortured man in the barn, even as she now slowly lowered herself into a cushioned seat at the long, farmhouse table in the dining room. The blinds had all been closed—understandable given that they overlooked the barn.

The man's widow didn't sit across from them, but rather stood, arms crossed, head high as if in some sort of military posture. She frowned at Ilse and Sawyer where they watched her from over steaming brews of unsweetened tea which she had offered when they'd set foot in the house.

Ilse glanced back towards the end of the hall, through the mud room towards where her shoes sat neatly by the door. *No shoes in the house.* That had been Mrs. Jackson's first comment.

Sawyer rubbed a hand through his hair, letting out a long, leaking sigh. "So you found him, huh?" Sawyer said.

Mrs. Jackson watched him, her features gaunt, her expression severe. Her eyes were dry, but everything about her seemed in shock, from the dilation in her pupils, to the faint trembling of her left hand pressed to her elbow, to the way she kept asking them the same question.

"Can I get you some tea?" she murmured for the third time, a far-off stare in her eyes. She blinked a couple of times, then glanced towards the steaming mugs in front of the agents. "Oh," she murmured. "Right."

"Please," Ilse said, gesturing towards a chair across the table. "Have a seat."

The woman flinched and shook her head. "No, no I'd rather stand."

Sawyer glanced at Ilse then back at the woman. "You found your husband, yes?"

Mrs. Jackson swallowed, but then nodded. "I—I, yes. I found him." She stared off again, at the window, even though the blinds were shut. "I—I didn't recognize him at first," she murmured. "It was so horrible." She blinked, glancing towards Sawyer. "Would you like some tea?" she murmured, but she didn't wait for a response, and instead continued as if answering to some unspoken question. "I—I heard sounds from the barn. Thought one of the hounds must have gotten out. I went to investigate with a flashlight and then... then..." Instead of getting more emotional, her voice only numbed further. "I found him dangling there," she said simply. "Blood dripping everywhere. His eyes were open... Staring at me."

She trailed off, glancing into the distance and then releasing the faintest huff. Ilse spotted the woman's hands both trembling violently. One hand, gripping a steam mug of her own by the handle, sent sloshing liquid over the edge of the thing. The liquid hissed where it struck the top of the lacquered farmhouse table.

"Do you know the names," Sawyer started, raising his phone, "Adelaide Stevens or Arthur Lehman?"

The woman frowned, glancing towards the pictures on the phone. She waited, considering her response carefully, studying the photos, then looked up. "Never seen them before in my life. Did they do this?"

Sawyer just shook his head.

"Did your husband have any enemies, ma'am?" Ilse asked. "Did anyone threaten him?"

The woman seemed to snap out of her reverie at this question, and her eyes narrowed as she stared at Ilse. "He had nothing *but* enemies. He made a mistake years ago. It's haunted him forever."

"What sort of mistake?" Sawyer pressed.

"You know," she retorted. "You undoubtedly looked him up when you got here."

"He's on the registry," Sawyer asked.

The woman just scowled. "Like I said, he made a mistake. He served his time in that hellhole of a prison. And now he keeps paying for it for the rest of his life. My husband had many enemies. Not the least of which wore badges like yours. Now please, I've said what I know. You need to leave."

Sawyer hesitated, then got slowly to his feet.

Ilse paused long enough to murmur, "You said you heard sounds. What sort of sounds?"

"I couldn't say. I wasn't paying attention. Good evening, agents."

The woman then turned, marched stiff-legged towards the door, her long dress swishing, and opened the door, pointing a finger angrily out into the night.

Ilse got slowly to her feet as well, the chair creaking beneath her. Sawyer allowed her to move first. Together, they both nodded farewell to the widow and moved into the darkness. The door *thumped* shut behind them, leaving them on the porch to the ranch house.

Sawyer ran a hand through his sandy hair, causing his cap to tilt forward. "No connections then," he muttered, glancing at her. "Old farmer. Didn't know the other victims. Different career, different age bracket, different appearance."

"Maybe his criminal past is related," Ilse said.

"Maybe. But how does that connect the first two victims? If anything, there are fewer connections than before."

Ilse put a hand against a load-bearing wooden beam of the porch. She looked out across the dark land, in the opposite direction of the barn and red and blue flashing lights.

"Maybe there are no connections," she said. "Maybe he's killing at random."

"Hmm."

"You think so?"

"Huh."

"Sawyer, hello," Ilse waved a hand towards her partner who was also staring off, but only as far as his fingers, which he'd curled, as if examining his nails. "Hey—Earth to Sawyer! You there?"

He looked up suddenly, blinking as if jolting from a nap. He stared at her, frowned, then said. "What was that?"

"Are you okay?"

He waved a hand distractedly. "Fine, fine. Look—we have no leads, it's getting late. Best call it a night and start fresh in the morning."

Ilse hesitated, glancing at Sawyer, but then looking quickly back in the direction of the barn so he wouldn't catch her staring. She wasn't sure why he was behaving so distractedly. He seemed even gruffer than usual. Standing next to him, he still smelled of sawdust. A farm like this seemed far more suited to a man like Sawyer than any FBI office.

And yet he stood out of place here, too, after a fashion.

This whole case was just sad. A woman who'd been born with less than pleasant features—she'd volunteered to have her features altered by surgery. A man who'd committed a grave crime who'd tried to start over, but never really managed it. Another man, completely different, who was a marathon runner—an athlete.

So much wasted life. The bleak skies seemed a fitting testament.

"I'll find my own way back," Ilse said quietly, stepping down from the porch and using the thick, wooden stairs. They looked, judging by the screws and the slight angle of the rails, to have been homemade.

"You sure?"

"Yeah. One of the officers can drive me back."

"City is like two hours away."

Ilse shook her head. "It's fine. I'll rest, don't worry."

Sawyer watched her for a moment, but then shrugged once, patted her on the back with a warm hand, then began strolling up the dusty road, his thumbs hooked in his belt loops. As he moved away, head downturned, quiet as ever, Ilse's gaze flitted back in the direction of the silo with the missing vines.

What did a soybean farmer have in common with a red-haired marathon runner? What did a fashion model have in common with either?

Something had to connect them, didn't it? The first two victims had died in the city. But this latest one was a hundred miles away...

It didn't make sense.

Sawyer reached their car parked on the side of the road. Ilse gave a faint wave which he returned in the form of a nod as he slipped into the seat and spun the wheel, kicking up dust as he tore away from the farm.

Ilse double-checked the number of police cruisers around the farm. She'd have to speak with one of the sergeants to make sure she wasn't left stranded.

But she didn't want to drive with Sawyer. Not now. He carried an aura now... a strange sense. She couldn't quite place it. Was he still thinking about his sister? Was he regretting telling Ilse about any of it?

She stared at the silo, at the missing vines...

Why vines?

There had been rope in the barn. She'd seen it. Cable as well.

Why vines?

She'd read the arrest report for Mr. Jackson. It didn't have anything to do with the assault. Almost as if the killer hadn't cared.

If anything, Mr. Jackson had managed to carve a life out for himself. He'd served his time in prison... Most of Ilse's clients weren't nearly so lucky. Men like Jackson preyed on people who came to Ilse for help. Many of them, over time, were given freedom from the shame, the horror... Others, though, remained stuck for years... forever...

Ilse herself, now in her thirties, still remembered the horrors of her childhood home, the lakeside house. The memories still haunted her. At least, the ones she didn't repress.

Thirty years was a long time to take from another soul.

And yet the soybean farmer was trying... trying to rebuild, trying to reroute, trying to end better than he started...

She frowned at this thought, stepping into the middle of the dusty road, hands in her pockets, her sweater sleeves bunched at her hips. She stared at the barn. Then she turned, looking over the soybean stalks through the fields.

The vines... the beans...

Jackson.

Jack.

She snorted to herself and shook her head faintly. Smiling at the silly idea. "Whatever, Beck," she muttered. "Dream on..."

But even as she thought it, she felt a faint prickle of something... some sort of realization. As if her subconscious was just trying to whisper.

She took another step towards the barn. A red-headed runner... Ginger? That's what some people called red hair. A ginger runner.

"No...," she murmured. "No... you can't be serious..."

A cold chill now spread across her skin. Her eyes suddenly widened as she thought of Adelaide. The ugly little girl turned pretty princess... Suddenly, the prickle turned into a buzz. Adele's eyes bulged. Her hand almost darted for her phone. But she paused, just standing in the road, her mind spinning.

It wasn't possible, was it? It couldn't be...

Unless... Unless it was...

But she couldn't call Sawyer. Not now. Not yet. It was just a hunch. A crazy, ridiculous hunch. A coincidence at the most, but still... She needed to get home. To do some of her own research. But what if she was right? What if the murders didn't just fit a pattern—what if the pattern was so obvious it was practically screaming?

"Officer!" she called suddenly, waving towards a man by the barn doors. "Officer, I need a ride back into Seattle!"

CHAPTER FOURTEEN

Tom Sawyer didn't much like thinking of Rebekah. Didn't much like remembering her face. But when he slept, it wasn't like he had an option. Most his dreams were the same. Dreams were shitty things. Too much imagination. Tom had never considered himself a fanciful person. Some people hated black and white. He preferred it to color. Color was distracting;color hid its meanings. He was a man of the dust and the dirt and the trees and the churning rivers coming from melted snowdrifts in mountains.

He was not a fanciful man.

And yet the dreams always came, regardless of his preference. He could still remember everything about her. Her smile, the way she'd twist a strand of hair around one finger when she was lost in thought. The way her brow would scrunch, as it had since she'd been a child, when she was focusing on a particularly difficult question. She'd always asked questions, always had an inquisitive spirit.

She'd also looked up to her big brother, more than anyone.

The monster who'd taken her had known how to hurt Tom most. He'd loved his baby sister. She'd been his best friend for years—his only friend, really. She'd always had a way with people, like a light drawing moths. Others had flocked to her, had wanted to spend time in her presence. She'd exuded joy and delight. She hadn't been perfect, either. Sawyer wasn't the sort to recollect with blinders on. She'd had a temper, just like him. She'd been judgmental of others. Things had come so easy to her, and she hadn't understood why the same wasn't true for everyone.

She'd never known how smart she was. Never been willing to admit it or cut anyone else some slack for falling short of the lofty standards she kept herself to. She'd loved, she'd laughed, she'd served, she'd hurt, she'd sinned, she'd been everything a human was meant to be. Everything a little sister was.

And then he'd come.

He'd cut her to pieces to torment Tom.

And Sawyer had arrived too late.

He'd wanted to kill the man then, wanted to put him in the ground.

But his partners had held him back when they'd finally caught up with the monster.

And now he sat in prison.

Tom shifted on the bed, eyes closed, but seeing far more this way than when they were open. He tugged his comforter tightly around his shoulders and twisted the other way, his stomach aching as it so often did as if from hunger pangs.

But this was a type of hunger that couldn't be satiated with food.

No. Sawyer wanted something else entirely.

Something forbidden.

He sat up, breathing heavily in his small, single bedroom. He only had the one blanket, didn't use sheets. Preferred replacing the mattress than getting it cleaned. He didn't bother himself with such chores—it distracted from the job.

Breathing heavily, sweat dripping down his forehead, he stared off into the dark of his spartan bedroom, sparsely furnished with furniture of his own making. He'd built the wardrobe over a weekend. He'd built the nightstand as well from some old sinker redwood and epoxy. It was the nicest thing he owned.

Now, blankets bunched around his ankles, nostrils flared as he inhaled and exhaled rapidly, Sawyer felt slow chills along his spine.

The hunger he felt always came at night. And never left until he spent a few minutes breathing and thinking...

Not so much thinking... as fantasizing.

Perhaps he was more fanciful than he gave himself credit for.

But there was only one thing he focused on in moments like this.

Revenge.

The killer was in prison. The man who'd ruined his baby sister, who'd turned a soul into dust. That man was now behind bars. Where Sawyer couldn't reach him...

Yet.

But he was working on a plan. Was thinking it through. He didn't want to just kill the monster. He wanted to hurt him. For a very, very long time. He'd placed calls in the past to some of his friends in the prison system. Guards, and even a warden, had provided favors. Food revoked, solitary confinement without explanation, bunkmates who were particularly horrific.

But it still wasn't enough. Sawyer wanted to see the man. To look him in the eyes.

He gritted his teeth at the thought, wondering what Doctor Beck might think of how dark his thoughts often went. He rubbed at his arms, shivering, and then kicked at the blankets, sending them to the floor and rolling off the mattress.

He stood naked, sweating, his eyes blazing. His body had more than its fair share of scars—gifts from the many cases he'd taken and bad guys he'd taken down.

Black and white. Good and bad.

Ilse thought in color. For her job she needed to.

Sawyer didn't. For his, he couldn't afford the luxury.

As he stood there, inhaling slowly, allowing the residue of his imagination to flit through his mind, his phone suddenly began to ring.

Sawyer frowned, pulling the device from his discarded jeans crumpled at the base of the bed. He studied the name, then the digital clock on the screen.

Only five AM.

His alarm was set for five-thirty, but he rarely needed it these days.

The name of the phone, though, gave him a jolt of admiration. Dr. Beck was up even before he was. He was feeling uncomfortable around her in recent days. Uncomfortable with how much he'd told her, shown her. Uncomfortable with how much he'd revealed. It wasn't a question what he was going to do with his sister's murderer. It was only a matter of time.

Ilse would only get in the way. She had an overactive conscience at times. He respected her for it but mistrusted her just the same.

Sometimes, a conscience was only like a stick in spokes.

He lifted the phone, slowing his breathing, trying to clear his mind as if worried Ilse might sense his thoughts over the phone. "Doc?" he said on answer.

"Sawyer?" came a breathy reply. "Sawyer, I think I've got something! I think I've got it!"

He frowned, wincing. "You sound chipper."

"Oh—umm, yeah. Coffee. Lots of coffee," she said. "Look, forget about—"

"You sleep?"

"A little. Sawyer I think it's storybooks."

"What?"

Her voice was excited now, still motor-mouthing through her sentences, carried on by a second wind from a sleepless night as adrenaline met the benefits of caffeine.

"Stories!" Ilse declared over the phone so loudly he winced and lifted the device a bit away from his ear.

"What are you talking about?"

"The farmer's name was Jackson! Jack!"

He didn't reply. Just breathing and waiting.

"Are you still there?"

"Mhmm."

"Don't you see? A soy*bean* farmer named Jack?"

Again, he just waited, starting to get annoyed.

"Sawyer?"

"I'm here," he said testily. "Just waiting for you to start making sense."

"Jack and the beanstalk, Sawyer! The vines from the silo. He took the vines." Ilse was breathless now, but she kept going. "The model and her family, remember? She grew up homely but made herself beautiful. It's the Ugly Duckling!"

Sawyer slowly reached down for his clothing. He didn't mind wearing the same outfit two days in a row as long as it was somewhat clean.

"That," he said, as he pulled on his pants, "is insane. You know that, yeah?"

"Yes, yes," she said testily. "Insane—but so is the killer. It makes sense."

"I'm not so sure it does, Ilse," he said, exhaling through his nose and trying not to let his irritation show. He wasn't normally an irritated man. He was stubborn. There was a difference. And he liked Ilse, liked the way she thought outside the box. She wasn't trapped in the style of thinking so many agents were trapped in from rote memorization of case work.

But she was also fanciful.

"What about the runner?" Sawyer said. "Pinocchio?"

"No! Think about it. He had red hair! A ginger!"

"So?"

"It's the gingerbread man," she said, and he detected a sheepish note to her voice. Before he could reply with incredulity, she quickly added, "I know how it sounds. I know, I know, I know. Just think about it, though. People kill for way less. We caught a guy trying to recreate his father's abuse at an auction house. It doesn't *have* to make sense to us. It just has to make sense to them."

"Ilse, I don't really give a shit about *them.* So you're saying the marathon runner was..."

"Run, run as fast as you can...," Ilse said quickly. "I was just looking up the stories. You can't catch me, I'm the gingerbread man. See? It fits!"

Sawyer just blinked, standing shirtless, with the phone against his face. He waited for the words to linger, to allow the silliness of the claim itself to do its own work and make itself apparent. Some things didn't require much help in this arena.

Ilse seemed to sense his reluctance. "Just think about it, okay? Please? Jack and the Beanstalk, the Ugly Duckling and the Gingerbread Man. Our killer is recreating fairy tales and murdering the protagonists of the stories."

"Why?" Sawyer said, still keeping his irritation in check for Ilse's sake. He didn't really want to humor her, but in the past, he'd been served well by doing just that.

"I—I don't exactly know the *why.* But he's killing characters from fairy tales. I would bet anything."

"I don't know Ilse..."

"Do you have another theory that fits? Do you?"

Sawyer paused, bit his lip, then rolled his shoulders, exhaling a breath towards the ceiling. "Fine," he muttered. "It fits. What do you want to do about it?"

"I—I think if we can place which stories he's reenacting, we might be able to discover who he's going to target next. Maybe narrow based on name or career."

"What do you mean, exactly?"

Ilse gave a long sigh. "I'm... I think we need to research not just the stories, but the collections of stories. I've found books online where all three of these fairy tales appear in the same compilation, among others. What if he's working them sequentially? We could find out the next story if we find the right storybook..."

She waited now, trailing off. He could practically detect the wince on her face. It was a silly idea, but also, she was right, it did fit. Hadn't Ilse earned some latitude? One day, he was going to ask for that very same thing. Latitude.

Then forgiveness.

What could it hurt, anyway?

"Fine," he said. "We can look into it. Where do you want to meet up?"

"I'm at a coffee shop," she said. "I'll text you the address."

"You know a coffee shop open at five?"

"Opens at six, but I used to teach the owner's brother. That's not important. You can meet me. Does that work?"

"Mhmm. Shoot a text. See you then, doc."

He hung up, groaning and stretching before reaching for a new shirt inside his closet. The same color as the one he'd worn the day before. This one, at least, he hadn't used in his workshop recently, so it didn't smell of sawdust.

He slowly pulled on a t-shirt, then the flannel, buttoning it with shaking fingers. He frowned at the way his hands trembled.

Sometimes, he simply couldn't place the source of an emotion. He had them; he knew that much. But finding the root of his emotions took too much work, too much thinking. So he just snorted in disgust and buttoned his shirt trembling.

Emotions could wait. He didn't mind following this lead with Ilse, if it could be called that. But spending more time with her? He winced...

It was growing uncomfortable. It was frustrating him. He shouldn't have told her about Rebekah. Shouldn't have mentioned the murder.

Of all the people to let into that part of his life, why the hell had he chosen a shrink?

Because you can trust her. Because she's kind.

He frowned at the thought. Trust? He couldn't trust anyone. Trust was earned. And no one managed to meet the standards required. Not just his standards, but Rebekah's. If he'd trusted less, if he'd trusted himself, his gut, she might still be alive.

Still... he was assigned to the case with Ilse and couldn't avoid it.

He would just keep his mouth shut now, his thoughts to himself. They were going to look up fairy tales after all. How hard could it be?

CHAPTER FIFTEEN

Ilse took a long sip from the cooling espresso sitting in the small, wooden holder in front of her. Sawyer had opted to sit at different booth, off to the side. He'd cited proximity to the outlet, but Ilse wasn't so sure.

For now, though, she was too focused. She'd borrowed the laptop from the agency and was now scanning the results on her search page.

The coffee shop was small and exuded the familiar fragrance, primarily of the drip brew the local shop was known for. Due to the early nature of their attendance, morning commuters came in and out, fetching their daily dose of energy in egg-carton textured cup holders. The tables themselves were made of what looked like driftwood coated in some protective finish. The chairs and booth seats were comfortable and padded with crimson plastic.

Sawyer was staring at his computer screen, his eyes glazed, his baseball cap sitting on the table next to his mouse. His tousled hair jutted every which way, suggesting he hadn't taken a comb to it that morning.

She tried not to stare at her partner, but it was a difficult thing to stay focused. He seemed to be ignoring her, or at the very least distancing himself. He hadn't taken to the search with the same gusto she had.

Ilse's brow flitted down, but she returned her attention to the search engine on her borrowed device.

Her theory sounded crazy.

She knew that.

But she was confident in it, nonetheless. Too much fit for it all to be pure coincidence. Now, she'd been up most of the night reading fairy tales and researching origins of the stories, as well as compilations.

But so far, it hadn't provided a lead-worthy clue. None of it would help if it didn't point her to the identity of the killer, or, at the very least, the identity of his next victim. Which fairy tale would he mimic next? This was what she was looking for.

She clicked on a link, and frowned, cycling through pictures on a website. "Did you know," she murmured, "they have Renaissance fairs for this stuff?"

Sawyer glanced over. "Huh?"

"Yeah. Conventions, handmade crafts, fashion design. They sell fairy wings—hundred bucks a pop."

Sawyer's eyebrows went up. "I found a fairy school," he said dryly, turning his screen towards her.

Ilse winced. "Ah, alright then. You think that's connected somehow?"

He looked her dead in the eyes. "Not even a little bit."

She rolled her own eyes, snorting and turning back to her screen. "You seem distracted again, Tom. Is everything alright?"

"Hmm? Fine."

"You sure?" she said, not making eye contact. A trick she'd learned in counseling had been styles of confrontation. Women, oftentimes, could be spoken to face to face, across a table, or over a Zoom meeting. They were connected on a personal level, interested in the emotions of others and so would be willing to go deep across from another.

Many men, on the other hand, didn't do well with confrontation. A parenting technique for young boys was often to take them for a drive rather than seat them at the kitchen table for a reprimand. Facing towards a road, with the person at one's side, both looking away from the other, helped to offset the sense of confrontation.

Whereas plopping them at a kitchen table across from looming parents would yield rebellion and defensiveness. Sawyer was much in this second category.

Ilse refused to look in his direction, preferring to face across the coffee shop, in the same direction as Sawyer. Her attention, visibly, seemed fixed on her screen. But once more, she was watching Sawyer like a hawk out of the corner of her eye.

"You haven't been yourself," she said simply, still not looking at him. She didn't phrase it as a question. Sometimes, allowing clients to come to their own conclusions was a far more helpful path. Other times, observations made as statements prompted more direct replies. Sawyer had always appreciated direct.

"Hmm," he said.

"You're moody and distracted. You don't have to tell me what's wrong. But it might help us do the work better."

Again, meeting him on his level. Sawyer liked work—he was married to the job. Something his ex-wife, Jennifer, could attest to.

"We're doing fine," he retorted. "I'm looking into fairy schools."

This time, he couldn't keep the sarcasm from his voice. Ilse looked at him now, frowning. "You don't have to mock my idea, you know," she said. "You can tell me what's wrong, or pretend nothing is, but I'm not your punching bag."

Sawyer blinked and scratched at his chin. He wasn't the sort to apologize, but she could tell he felt bad. He glanced around, noted her nearly empty cup and said, "Want another?"

She shook her head and hid a smile. "Yes, please. Thank you. And I forgive you."

Sawyer just snorted, got to his feet and moved towards the register.

Ilse turned back to her screen. She couldn't focus both on Sawyer *and* the case, and for the moment, the stakes in the latter were much higher. At least, so she hoped. People were dropping like flies. She had to focus.

She hunched a bit, scowling at her computer screen. The killer was clearly basing his murders off of the stories... So the stories themselves had to be key. But the stories weren't ending in ever after. The killer was *changing* the endings, intentionally.

But why? Was that the key?

She clicked on a tab beneath the search bar, navigating back to a sales page for a compilation of fairy tales.

The murderer didn't like the happy endings, so he was changing them. Killing the protagonists of the tales. Was that it? Some sort of envy, or jealousy? Or something deeper?

Why was he altering the fairy tale endings? Was the man trapped in his own youth, somehow? Had his maturation been stilted? Most likely—fairy tales weren't often key landmarks of the psyches for adults. At least, not without multiple layers obscuring childhood narratives.

She stared at the screen, and then her eyes flicked down, and she frowned.

Beneath the picture of the compilation, she spotted a row of advertised products and then recommended books. One of the advertisements simply read, *Read local authors!*

The picture above the title was a very poor image from a horribly crafted book cover. Like someone with little know-how had tried to piece something together in Microsoft Paint. Paint was the extent of Ilse's own graphic design acumen.

She stared at the photo of the bad cover. Stared at the blurb. Read local authors!

A demand. Local authors?

She clicked.

The poor covers, judging by the reviews, also carried poor stories. She scrolled down to the sales rank of the story, noting that it hadn't performed particularly well, seeing as it ranked somewhere in the lowest rungs on the online retailer's website.

She scrolled back up, reading the book's description.

It simply said, *How they should have ended...*

She clicked to the reviews, reading them slowly, her frown deepening like grooves in clay. All the reviewers seemed to be complaining about the same things. The book was titled *Fairy Tales,* simple enough. But according to the reviewers, they all ended in disaster.

One reviewer said, *"I picked this up to read to my daughter before bed. That was until I reached the end of the first tale. Everyone dies! Horrible. One star. Do* not *recommend."*

Other reviews expressed similar sentiment. A few five-star reviews read things like, "*Lots of blood. Love it!"*

Another one of the rare positive reviews said, "*Turning children's stories into horror—just my thing!*"

Ilse frowned, clicking to the main page again. The author's name was listed as Roy Clement. She clicked his bio, reading it slowly. Roy had moved to Seattle, it seemed, from San Francisco five years ago. Before becoming a writer, apparently, according to his bio, he'd worked at a prestigious studio adapting fairy tales. The way he spoke of the studio, though, in the biography, was hardly in flattering terms. He phrased it to maximize a sense of his talent while minimizing a sense of the studio's competence.

Had he been fired? Was that what had prompted the move?

And now, years later, he was writing stories that failed to sell whatsoever.

She clicked on the author's page and frowned at a picture of Mr. Clement. Perhaps it was all the time she'd spent studying online books over the last few hours, but in her mind, Mr. Clement looked a bit like Humpty-Dumpty. He had an egg-shaped, bald head, and oversized eyes that almost seemed to be bulging from their sockets.

He was smiling, but it was a weak attempt at the gesture.

Something tapped next to her hand, and a sudden gust of steam swept across her face. She blinked, looking over to see Sawyer having placed the new coffee next to her. He frowned over her arm at the image on the screen.

"Who's that?" he said.

Ilse said, "Thanks," nudging the coffee, then said, "Not sure. But... But I'd like to speak with him."

"Oh? Suspect?"

"I'm again, not sure... but...," she stared at the image on the screen, frowning. "He re-writes fairy tales," she murmured, "turning them into bloody horror shows."

"Yeah?"

She looked up at Sawyer. "Also, he's local."

"Huh. You think he might know something?"

Ilse glanced back at the author page and the published books beneath the photograph. "He's changed the endings of the Ugly Duckling and Jack and the Beanstalk. Killed them both in this tale here."

"What are those two stars?"

"Those?" Ilse said. "Reviews. It didn't do very well in that arena."

"Huh."

"Right. Huh."

"Fine," Sawyer said. "I'll call Rudy. See if he can get us an address. You sure he's local?"

"That's what the ad said. Also, what his bio states."

Sawyer stepped away from the table, fishing his phone from his pocket now. Ilse, for her part, slowly lowered the lid of her laptop, frowning faintly to herself. Someone was turning happily ever after into a horror show.

Roy Clement seemed the perfect culprit.

CHAPTER SIXTEEN

Ilse was satisfied to sit passenger-side as Sawyer drover her through the city. “Rudy isn't calling back,” Sawyer said with a frown, his hands wrapped around the steering wheel.

A sudden dinging noise echoed in the car.

“Was that...,” Sawyer hesitated. “That wasn't mine.”

Ilse paused, then reached for her own phone in surprise. She pulled the device from her pocket, adjusting the seatbelt across her chest, and lowering her gaze from the windshield to look at her phone. “Oh,” she said suddenly. “I think he just texted me—I didn't know Rudy had my number.”

Sawyer snorted but didn't say anything.

Ilse winced. “Huh. Yeah... I guess that was a dumb comment.”

“Rudy has *everyone's* number,” Sawyer muttered. “What did he say?”

Ilse frowned at the message, clearing her throat. “Cleaning up some of the language,” she said in a clipped tone, “he says, and I quote, *come on kids—you don't need me for this. Look at the dude's website, my dear! Now let daddy get his nap.*”

Sawyer glanced at Ilse, his lips curving into the faintest smile which he tried to hide just as quickly. “What was that last part again?”

“The website part?”

“No, the other part. It just sounds so strange coming from your lips.”

Ilse snorted. “Guess we should check Mr. Clement's website, hmm?”

Sawyer kept one hand on the wheel, steering them through traffic as they moved towards a main road, and with his other he fished his phone from his pocket and handed it to Ilse. She accepted the device, and—with some instruction—found the internet browser and searched for the local would-be author's name.

The website came up slowly and looked like something from the nineties. Ilse tried to click on a couple of links, but they all lead to dead pages. On the front page, however, she spotted something that caught her attention.

"He does events," she murmured.

"The author does?"

"Yes. Events—he's hosting one today. That must have been what Rudy meant."

Sawyer frowned. "What time? Where?"

"At a booth," Ilse replied. "At a local convention..." She clicked over to the webpage for the convention itself, a much more sleek, up-to-date site. She read the intro and then said, "It looks like a sort of fantasy convention in a conference room at the Autumn Hotel."

"Huh."

"What?"

"What's that?"

"A fantasy convention?"

"Mhmm."

Ilse shrugged. "According to the website it's a place where people gather to enjoy fantasy, I guess. Some local authors will be there. Looks like some actor. I don't watch TV, but I guess she's a pretty big deal."

"Forget about the actress. Autumn Hotel, you said? What time?"

Ilse glanced at the phone again then looked up. "There's an event every other Saturday—it's already started but goes for half the day. We still have time."

Sawyer muttered to himself, but retrieved his phone and, eyes bouncing up and down from road to screen, programmed the GPS. He attached it to the suction on the windshield and then picked up the speed, following the thin, purple line on the device as it led them in the direction of the fantasy convention. And towards the location of the horror writer.

***

Ilse wanted to scan the conference hall, but she was having far too much fun simply watching Sawyer's expression. His eyes were wide beneath his baseball cap. His sleeves were rolled back, and his jeans—the same jeans he'd worn the previous day—had a coffee stain on the thigh. The man's calloused hands were hooked through his belt loops, and he was muttering beneath his breath. "Unbelievable."

A fully armored knight walked past, tipping a gauntleted hand to his metal visor. "Hello," an echoing voice said from within the costume. The knight continued on his way, clanking with the plastic and metal armor as he moved towards a table display.

More than a hundred folks had already arrived at the conference, and all of them were dressed in fairy cosplay or as knights and creatures from magical stories.

Judging by Sawyer's expression, he thought he was hallucinating.

"What was in that coffee?" he muttered. "Ilse... pinch me."

She obliged, and he took his hat off to fan his face. "This is all... a bit much, isn't it?"

Ilse patted Sawyer on the same arm she'd playfully pinched. "You'll survive," she said with a chuckle. "Stop staring at everyone. You're weirding them out."

"I'm weirding *them...*," Sawyer trailed off, shaking his head.

A woman wearing a tall, towering pink wig with butterfly barrettes and glitter batted her long, fake eyelashes at Sawyer as she passed, adjusting the transparent straps of her gossamer wings.

Ilse nodded politely at the conference-goer, but then began to lead Sawyer through the costumed cosplayers. If their killer was hiding among those in outfits, they'd never spot him. He'd blend right in. Perhaps this was how he'd found his previous victims—she'd have to check to see if they'd shared an interest in fantasy.

As Ilse moved through the booths, past tables with placards identifying the contents, she spotted two young men arguing behind one of the tables. Both men were pointing at each other, saying things like:

"I rented the spot last week. I didn't *need* to confirm."

"Take it up with the host! My name is on the table. So it's mine."

The two men both wore bright, bedazzled outfits. One of them had a knight's helmet, the other's face was sweaty beneath a tricorn hat with silver tassels. They were both pointing towards the table. One man stood protectively next to a box full of small, sixth-scale figurines. Another had stacks of comic books he was trying to arrange on the table. Every time he placed a comic, though, the second man grabbed it and pushed it back in the small carry-on case the first fellow was using.

"Stop touching them!" the man with the comics yelled. "You'll smudge them!"

The second man just sneered and said, "Go away. Find your own table."

Ilse's eyes moved past the men, landing on a figure sitting at the far end of the arrangement, behind the smallest booth.

She froze.

The fellow was watching his bickering neighbors with a mild smile, as if the irritation caused him enjoyment. But at the same time, he kept glancing hopefully at passing conference-goers. None of them stopped in front of his table, however.

A small pile of books carried the same covers Ilse had seen online.

The man was bald, with bugging eyes. He wore a bowtie and a suit made of fake leaves and branches.

"There," Ilse murmured beneath her breath to Sawyer, pointing towards the seated fellow.

The two of them made a beeline for the man, stepping past the table with the bickering patrons and coming to a halt in front of the author's booth.

"Hello!" the man said cheerfully, beaming now. "Interested in a gripping story with a clever twist?"

Ilse cleared her throat. "I'm afraid not, sir."

The man took in their outfits, glancing at Sawyer's flannel to Ilse's sweater. His smile dimmed a few watts. "Do I know you...," he said slowly.

"FBI," Sawyer muttered, shooting an irritated glance to the arguing men at the second booth. "We need to ask you a few questions.

Clement's eyes bugged, even more than they had at first. "I—F—What? Shit—what's this about?"

Sawyer shook his head. "How about we go somewhere a bit more quiet, hmm?"

The author behind the table had frozen in place. His hands were flat against the table, the knuckles white. He stammered again, shaking his head faintly. "I—I don't have to go anywhere with you!" he protested. "You have *no right!*"

Sawyer frowned, stepping closer. "We need to speak with you, sir."

The bug-eyed man glanced to Ilse then back, prickles of sweat on his forehead. One of his hands moved towards a book, gripping it as if preparing to use it like a club.

Just then, the comic-book owner shouted. "I said stop smudging them!" He threw a punch. A pathetic, weak, looping thing. More a slap, or a flail, really.

But he scored a blow on the other man's shoulder. This second fellow yelped as if he'd been shot and shoved the first man back. One of the fairy-women screamed.

Distracted, Sawyer glanced towards the aggressors. "Cut it out," Sawyer snapped. "Before I come over there—ah shit. Hey, hey stop!"

But Mr. Clement had taken the opportunity presented. His chair toppled as he made good his getaway, sprinting in the opposite direction, towards a side exit door.

Sawyer was already breaking into a sprint as well, vaulting the table, and sending the books scattering. Ilse moved around the table, taking after the two men.

Her heart reached her throat, and her stomach churned. Another conference-goer screamed, someone shouted something. The two men fighting near the comic-book table were yelling back and forth as others arrived to try and separate them.

Their would-be suspect, though, reached the exit first, slamming a shoulder into the door. The fire alarm started blaring in the morning calm.

Sawyer grunted, slamming through the door a second later, his long legs carrying him rapidly forward. Ilse followed close behind, panting. She glimpsed the heel of the author disappear up a flight of stairs as Sawyer flung the exit open, and together, the two agents gave rapid pursuit.

CHAPTER SEVENTEEN

Two women, dressed in ballroom gowns both squawked as Mr. Clement barreled between them, knocking them over, petticoats flying.

Ilse winced and shouted, "Sorry!" as she jumped over one of the sprawling women and hastened up the stairs. Sawyer had stopped to catch the second woman before she fell and hit her head. "You good?" he said. "Good!" He pushed past her, racing up the steps as well.

The faint delay had cost him time, though. Now, Ilse was in the lead, gasping and panting as she raced after Mr. Clement.

"Stop!" she yelled up the stairs. "Stop now! FBI!"

"Leave me alone!" a moaning voice, carried by a panting breath came from above. She watched pale fingers slapping against the banister above as she curled around the stairs as well and followed up the next flight.

The man didn't appear to be armed—didn't appear to be much of a threat at all. As she hastened up the stairs, two at a time, sweating, breathing heavily, taking one flight, two, three, she found their suspect was now leading them higher up the hotel, away from the conference room.

She heard a clatter from above, a yelp. And then spotted red liquid pooling down the steps on the fourth-floor landing.

Her heart pounded as she reached the landing and she spotted a man, wearing an outfit like a pirate leaning against the wall, massaging his head. A tray of drinks had been sent smashing to the floor, red liquid—which smelled like strawberries—glazing the ground.

Ilse hopped the puddle, lunging for a slowly closing door at the top of the staircase.

"He's heading into the hotel!" she shouted over her shoulder. She paused long enough to check the man in the pirate outfit. "Are you alright?"

He massaged his head, wincing, red liquid dripping from his fingertips. "I—I think I'm stabbed... wait—no... No just the drinks. Shit—what was that?" the man turned, shouting through the door Ilse now held open. "You hooligan!"

Sawyer had now caught up with Ilse, and the two of them shoved hastily into the hallway of the fourth floor.

That's when Ilse spotted him. Mr. Clement was standing at the end of a long hall, near two large windows, staring out into the morning with a horrified expression on his face. He shot a frightened look back, then returned his attention to the window.

That's when Ilse realized what he intended.

"Scaffolding," she said sharply.

"Saw it," Sawyer replied.

The two agents approached slower now. Red footprints, from the sticky drink, led from the door, down the hall, towards where the would-be author was standing, a dazed look in his eyes.

"I didn't do anything!" he screamed. "Leave me alone!" He reached up then, opening the window and staring towards the painting scaffolding. He took a long puff of air, then stepped up, placing one foot on the windowsill.

He looked back again, eyes wide with panic.

Sawyer made a guttural growl, stomping down the hallway now and approaching the man with his foot on the window sill.

"You won't," Sawyer snapped. "You want to fall and die? Hmm? Nah—you won't."

"Stay back!" the man screamed. "Get away from me!"

"You're wanted for questioning," Sawyer said, his tone as cold as the blood of a rattlesnake. "Get the hell off that sill. Come here. Now."

The man braced as Sawyer drew nearer still. He looked panicked in Ilse's direction, then back at Sawyer. A small sob escaped his lips and he leaned forward, trying to pull himself onto the window ledge. He gripped at the wooden painting scaffolding beyond.

"Don't do it," Ilse called in warning. "You'll fall."

The man was blubbering now, sobbing and shaking his head wildly. He gave a long rasping groan, the fake leaves of his suit crackling like plastic bags.

Sawyer just kept walking forward. Not running, not jogging—a simple, calm walk. He didn't seem at all perturbed by the man's posture. Ilse didn't know what they'd do if he tried to flee via scaffolding. If he fell from the fourth floor, he'd break most of the bones in his body.

The man looked back at Sawyer, who was still strolling forward, a frown affixed to his features. Mr. Clement shook a finger back over his shoulder. "Stay away! I'm warning you—stay back!"

Clearly, he hadn't reached the decision to climb the scaffolding yet, or else he would already have left. But now, facing out the window, staring at the plummet and the rickety, wooden structure, he seemed to have lost his nerve.

A nerve, though, that was quickly approaching the closer Sawyer got.

"Sawyer," Ilse said slowly, a warning note to her tone.

"Stay back!" Clement screamed.

"You won't," Sawyer muttered. "You just won't."

Ilse again, "Sawyer—careful. He's going—"

"I said to leave me alone!" Clement screamed. And then he lunged through the window, towards the scaffolding.

Sawyer didn't speak this time, but surged forward all of a sudden, closing the last few steps in leaping bounds.

He snatched a handful of fake green leaves in the makeshift suit, yanking *hard.* Mr. Clement shouted, Ilse braced herself, the window clattered. Something from the wooden painter's scaffolding cracked.

And then, Sawyer yanked the man bodily back through the window, flinging him towards the carpeted hotel hallway.

The man struck the ground with a grunt and a sound like a leaking balloon. He stared dazedly up at the ceiling, wincing and massaging at his ribs.

Sawyer pointed down at the man, growling, "We told you to stop."

The man tried to respond, but just wheezed again, moaning as he tried to sit up. But Sawyer caught him, spinning him onto his stomach and twisting his arm behind his back.

"Owowowow," the man protested with a shout.

Ilse had hastened to Sawyer's side now and she stooped quickly, cuffs in hand, grabbing the man's wrist and slipping the handcuff over it with a satisfying *click.*

"Sir, you're under arrest," she said firmly. "We need to ask you some questions."

***

The hotel had provided them with a small meeting room on the second floor. Ilse had agreed that the drive back to the precinct would have cost precious time. The killer had been striking every couple of days, which meant the more time wasted, the more danger someone was in.

But now, Ilse was hopeful, as she settled in the cushioned office chair, that they'd found their culprit.

She studied the man, frowning at him. He hunched in his seat, his cuffed hands resting on the table. He glared between the two of them, looking even more like Humpty-Dumpty than he had at first.

"I want a lawyer," the bald man demanded, mean-mugging both of them. "Now!"

Sawyer crossed his arms. "So you've said. Your lawyer has been notified. They're on their way."

"Good. I'm not saying shit."

Sawyer tapped his fingers against the table. "You like fairy tales, do you?" he paused as the words left his lips, and Ilse watched him swallow and give the faintest, incredulous shakes of his head as if he couldn't quite believe what he was saying.

"What?" the man snorted. "That's not a crime."

"No, no I suppose not," said Sawyer, watching the man. "Why'd you run?"

He leaned back in his chair, his face even more pale than the photo online in his author bio. He kept shooting nervous glances between the agents, inter-spliced by obnoxious shakes of his head or long glares.

"We have police heading to your home as we speak," Sawyer said simply. "If we find the murder weapon, plans, files on your computer—any of it. You're going away for a long time."

The man's eyes bugged, and he looked horrified. "You can't do that!" he protested loudly.

Sawyer leaned in, a bit more attentive all of a sudden. Sensing the same thing Ilse did.

Fear. This last comment had terrified their suspect.

"You ran and you tried to escape out a window," Sawyer said simply. "Why? What's got you spooked now? What are we going to find at your house, hmm? A knife? DNA evidence?"

"A—a knife.... what? No! No, you don't have permission to check my computers," he said, swallowing nervously. "Where's my lawyer?"

"On his way," Sawyer repeated.

Ilse, though, was staring at the man now, a frown etched across her brow. "Hang on," she murmured slowly. "What are you hiding on your computers?"

He looked at her now, panicked at every mention of the electronic device. "Nothing," he said, but his voice squeaked, and he swallowed a lump in his throat. "It's not—it's just... art... It's just art! That's all. I didn't do what you think I did! I don't even own a knife!"

"Everyone owns knives," Ilse said.

"No! No! You're talking like it's some sort of violent thing. I never hurt a fly. It's all just—just pictures! Shit, where's my lawyer!?" The failed animator was hyperventilating now, shaking his head so wildly sweat droplets scattered across the table.

Ilse studied the flustered man, trying to place the source of his terror. He didn't compute the references to violence, didn't even seem to care about the possibility they had him pegged for murder. Rather, he was terrified about his computer... About what they might find on it. Just pictures, he'd said. But what was he referring to?

"What are they going to find on your hard drive?" Ilse said quietly, staring at the man.

His bug eyes turned from Sawyer to her. "Nothing! Lawyer!"

Ilse leaned back, crossing her arms. "I see," she said slowly, feeling a sudden sense of frustration. As she stared at the man, she knew the truth.

This wasn't their guy.

Too scared. He ran instead of fought. When he had the chance, he didn't put up much of a struggle. This wasn't a violent man. He was a coward.

The leaf suit, the children's stories, the terror over his hard drive... Ilse closed her eyes and let out a faint sigh. "Ah... I *see,*" she repeated with a nod.

Sawyer glanced at her when she opened her eyes again and quirked an eyebrow in question.

"He has child pornography on his computer," she said matter-of-factly. She turned instantly to watch Mr. Clement's expression.

The pallor of his face would have made ghosts look tan by comparison. The sweat had now migrated from his forehead to his upper lip.

"They're just pictures!" he squeaked out.

Sawyer stared from Ilse to the man across the table in cuffs. "Come again?" he said.

"Underage pornography," Ilse said. "Just a guess, but confirmed by his reaction." She stood up in disgust, shaking her head. "You're wasting our time," she said, pointing an unyielding finger towards the man across the table. "And you're wasting your life," she added.

Sawyer stared at Clement from beneath hooded eyes. Ilse noticed the way his hands had bunched on the table. Her partner had a soft spot where children were concerned. And he had a much, much harder reaction towards those who victimized them, or enjoyed viewing their victimization like some sort of commodity.

"That's what we're gonna find?" Sawyer said, staring at the man.

Mr. Clement seemed to have noticed Sawyer's bunched fist as well now. "Lawyer," he squeaked again, shaking his head.

Just then, Sawyer's phone began to ring. He cursed, lifting the device and slapping it to his cheek. "What?" he demanded, his eyes blazing as he stared towards Mr. Clement. "Yeah. Yes. Second floor. Well send his ass up then, why don't you?"

He lowered the phone and made a snorting sound before shoving angrily to his feet.

This time, it was Ilse's turn to quirk a brow.

"His lawyer is here," Sawyer muttered, jutting a finger towards the man across from them. "Asshole's got legal on speed dial, I guess."

"The lawyer's heading up?"

"Yeah. Locals bringing him."

Ilse sighed, nodding. She reached out, gently pressing her fingers to Sawyer's wrist above his bunched hand.

The man was still sweating, trembling now, his handcuffs rattling under the close scrutiny.

"Don't like being watched, huh?" Sawyer muttered. "Not when you're vulnerable, I bet. Well get the hell used to it. Lotta people gonna watch you, Mr. Clement. No privacy for a while."

Ilse sighed, patting Sawyer on the arm, and thankfully he relaxed his fingers. She'd been worried he might punch the guy. She wanted to tell the man off as well, but she said, instead, "Get some help," in a soft voice. "Before it's too late." She gave a dejected shake of her head.

"I'll be right out in the hall," Sawyer added, pointing a finger towards the man behind the table. "I'll get you for this. Get you for the murders too."

A loud knock suddenly retorted on the wooden door. Sawyer glared beneath the brim of his cap as Ilse reached back, opening the door.

A woman in a business suit stood there, scowling at them. "What is this?" she demanded instantly.

Two cops were flanking her, looking sheepishly at the agents.

"We were holding him until you got here," Ilse said. "Needed immediate aid in an ongoing investigation."

"I don't care," the lawyer retorted. "You have no right to keep my client here. Is he under arrest?"

"Damn right he is," Sawyer snapped.

The lawyer looked at him, frowning. "What's your name? Badge number?"

Sawyer looked right back at her. "I forget." Then, he brushed past her, stomping out into the hall and leaving the office space.

Ilse passed a hand through her hair, then sighed, wincing towards the two officers who were watching the exchange. She also stepped into the hall, ignoring the pointed look from the lawyer. The door slowly shut behind her.

"Stay here," Ilse said, nodding towards the door. She looked from one local to the next. "Once they're done, take him to the station. Also, tell the locals searching his place to bring his hard drives. Got it?"

Both men nodded, and Ilse flashed a quick Okay sign before moving down the carpeted hall towards where Sawyer was stalking away. She had to jog to catch up with him.

As she did, Sawyer looked over at her. "Not our guy, is it?" he said glumly.

Ilse winced, shaking her head. "What clued you in?"

Sawyer lifted his phone, wiggling it. "Traffic report from his internet usage thanks to Rudy," Sawyer muttered. He glanced back at the device and lowered it again just as quickly. "Not sure I can stomach the site names."

"But it clears him?" Ilse asked, peering towards the printed screenshot on Sawyer's phone.

"Yeah," the tall man grunted, slowing his long gait to a slower stroll. He didn't look back down the hall towards the two posted officers either. "He was... busy. Active for hours during the first murder. Couldn't have done it."

"Right... He's not the type, either," Ilse said with a shrug. "If it's not him then..."

"So there goes the storybook theory," Sawyer said, turning now to face her. "Can't say I'm disappointed. Wasn't my favorite theory of yours if I'm honest."

Ilse though frowned. "The theory is good. The suspect isn't. They're different things."

Now Sawyer just looked at her incredulously. "You're not serious," he said.

Ilse returned the tenor of the stare. "As a heart attack. I'd stake anything that our killer is recreating fairy tales. We just need to try another angle."

Sawyer turned, snorting again and picking up the pace once more to stride down the hall.

"Don't you harrumph at me!" Ilse called after him. "I'm right about this."

"We caught a pervert not a killer, doc. We need a new option."

"No, we just need a different suspect, Tom."

"Whatever."

"Maybe," Ilse added, no longer walking after her partner but planting her feet firmly in the middle of the hall, "you'd see it too if you weren't so distracted."

"I'm not distracted!" he retorted, rounding on her with a glare. "I'm doing my job—you should try the same, doc." The moment he said it, he bit his lip, his jaw tensing. Both of them went still in the hall, fifteen or so paces separating the two of them.

Ilse frowned towards Sawyer, and he let out a faint sigh, jamming his hands into his pockets and looking off to the side like a chastised child.

"I'm also trying to do my job," Ilse returned, keeping her emotions in check. "And I believe the best way to do that is to stay the course. I don't appreciate your inference, Tom."

He gave a shrug. "Yeah. Yeah, that's fine. But I'm *not* distracted. I'm focused as ever, doc."

"If you say so." Ilse had long since learned how to control her emotions rather than giving into outbursts. She'd dealt with clients who sometimes went out of their way to get a rise out of her. She'd grown up in a family where fear or anger were choice delicacies. The more she showed them, the more she was provoked.

Now, her expression was impassive.

Sawyer refused to admit his head was in the clouds, or perhaps back home. Wherever it was, it certainly wasn't focused on the job at hand.

She knew it all sounded silly. Knew, also, that to be wrong would be a blight on her record. Not just with Sawyer but with Supervising Agent Rawley and the rest of the FBI. She wasn't thrilled to type up a report suggesting that fairy tales were the motive for murder.

But then again, she was convinced.

She had to stick to her guns.

And so she said, "I think our guy is still out there, and he's going to use a fairy tale as an excuse to strike again, Tom. If we don't stay the course, if we don't find him, then we're going to lose another. I know the theory is silly, but nothing else about this is silly at all. I know that. Can you trust me on that?"

Sawyer rubbed his jaw. "I trust you, doc," he said. But then he turned and began moving away again. As he left, he muttered beneath his breath, “And that's the problem...” He stalked away, through the door at the end of the hall and disappeared from sight.

Only once he was gone did Ilse stop to wish she'd asked *where* he was going.

A killer was out there. Sawyer was distracted, and Ilse had found a dead end. She knew fairy tales were the angle. But how could she get ahead of it all? She didn't know all the stories, didn't know their connections. Didn't know what to do next.

She waited a second longer, staring in the direction Sawyer had disappeared, then frowned, looking back towards where the two cops stood sentry.

She wasn't an expert on fairy tales. But behind that door... there was a man who was. Desperate times called for desperate measures. She rolled her shoulders, as if preparing for what came next, and then marched right back in the direction of the sealed office room door, a frown affixed to her features.

CHAPTER EIGHTEEN

He'd been watching these ones for a while, like a farmer tending fruit, waiting for it to ripen. And now they had.

He sat in his car, staring up at the small duplex at the end of the cul-de-sac. Figures moved across the windows, shadows flashing against the lights peering into the late afternoon. Morning, evening, night—he didn't care. Daylight didn't scare him. The eyes of others didn't alarm him. He would get what he wanted with or without witnesses.

And so far, everything had gone so smoothly.

This time, though, he was facing an entirely new challenge. Two protagonists instead of one. Double the price, double the trouble, double the reward. He had big plans for this one... The first tales had been short stories, but this would be his magnum opus. It required particular planning, particular execution. Every storyteller was known best for one piece of work.

He leaned over and pushed open the car door, remaining seated for the moment while adjusting the gloves on his hands. The vehicle was a rental, of course. He'd been more than careful.

He looked back in the direction of the duplex, watching as a thin figure moved across the front window, the glare of a TV smearing the glass. The sister, then. She was bone-thin, with curly brown hair. She wouldn't be the problem. No... It was the football player he had to look out for.

He massaged the corner of his jaw, wincing at the bruise forming there. The farmer had been a wild one—had fought and bucked like a bronco.

But Jack was dead. The giant lived.

These people didn't deserve their happy endings.

Hansel and Gretel would be next, and no amount of shrewd thinking or breadcrumbs in the woods would save them. He scowled in the dark, feeling old, putrid thoughts rising within. Happy endings didn't exist. Not really.

And those precious few who were allowed them, even they couldn't be permitted. Romance, friends, children, success, careers... it all boiled down to the way the story was told. The difference between a happy ending and a tragedy was simply where one put the period.

He'd learned that, hadn't he? At a very, very young age. He'd only had one friend locked in that attic. A friend in the form of a book. A dusty, worn, rough fairy tale book.

He reached over into the back seat, lifting the folded protective cloth covering and pulling the rectangular item into the front seat. He placed it on the passenger seat, and slowly unfolded it.

The green, dusty edge of a worn leather-bound storybook. He just stared at the familiar edge, tracing his fingers over the rough material. The texture brought memories back. His eyes widened, but he was no longer seeing inside his car, no longer looking towards the duplex.

All he could see now was *fate.*

His fate.

He could see the spiders climbing through their cobwebs. Could hear the moan of the wind against the shingles. Could feel his small, bony arms trembling as he shivered, freezing in that attic. Could hear the laughter below. Could feel his fingers straining, scraping, desperately scrabbling against the latch to the attack door.

Locked, though.

Always locked. And he'd been left upstairs. Left with his little book in the freezing attic with the spiders and the cockroaches and the stench of mothballs.

And the fear.

So much fear.

It had been a contradiction of realities, reading such stories while sitting in such a horrible place. He'd believed for years in happy endings. Had believed someone might come along and save him from that witch's house.

But no one came. No one saved him. He'd simply suffered. He'd cried out for help, cried out to God, cried out for the woman who'd locked him there. The witch herself.

But nothing changed. Things only worsened as he grew older.

"You're uglier now," he remembered her saying. *"And you're getting fatty fat."*

He frowned at the memory, his fingers still brushing the edge of the book. He could remember begging her to let him out of the attic. He remembered the way his bones had strained against his skin. He hadn't been fat nor ugly—he'd simply been older. He knew that now. But his mother had resented him for growing up. Had resented his childish features fading.

And while he'd tried to hide in children's stories, she'd hidden her child in the attic.

He'd survived, though it was a close thing. But something *had* died in that attic. The belief in happy endings, the belief that things would all work out for good in the end. The difference between a tragedy and a happy ending was simply the placement of the period.

And now he knew, with bone-deep certainty, that no one had a happy ending in store. He simply ushered them, far faster, into the inevitability of life. He gave them the gift of inciting labor prematurely.

He lifted his fingers from the book, his skin tingling as he did. He was surprised to find moisture in his eyes, and he reached up, wiping faintly at his cheeks, tracing the droplets of tears.

Then, chest pounding, he pushed open his car door, and stepped out into the catcalling night, beneath the wink of the moon and whistle of the wind.

He wasn't a monster, of course. He frowned, checking his gloves, adjusting them, and straightening his shoulders. He wouldn't hunt *children*—perish the thought. No, no, children had to grow up themselves, had to learn the stakes of reality. At least children, like him, had a chance of enlightenment.

These two, inside the duplex, a boy and a girl, had recently turned eighteen. The year of transformation. Crossing the threshold, the boundary, the final nail in the coffin of happy endings. They moved from hope to despair, life to death—they just didn't know it yet.

Eighteen was a good year to choose. Plus, missing children were much harder to hide. Adults got all up in a tizzy over missing kids. At least, some did. Other times, no one seemed to notice at all.

He scowled in the night, but then began stalking forward, hands flexed at his side as he neared the house, watching the shadows through the glass. The same rail-thin girl with springy hair moved past the blinds in the other direction now. Her head was glowing, and it took him a second to realize she had a phone pressed to her cheek and was prancing about the front room in her pajamas.

The woman shared an apartment with her twin brother. He'd already scoped the space out. The two of them were enrolled in a nearby university, which, of course, was where he'd gotten their information. Accessing a student website portal was the easiest thing he could think of.

He glanced back towards his car, clicking the locks and frowning before approaching the home. He circled around the back, stepping in the shadows cast by a large hedge and the eastern facing wall. Brickwork, or at least faux brickwork presented an unyielding form.

He checked the latch of the window into the bathroom. The same latch he'd shattered the previous night. And still, it remained broken.

He allowed himself a faint smile at a job well done.

The big bad wolf had arrived on the page. Fee-fi-fo, he smelled the blood of Hansel and Gretel just within these walls. He liked playing with his food, too. That was most the fun. A man had to find *some way* to amuse himself in this rotten world.

And so, with a faint grunt, and an askance glance back over his shoulder towards the street, he shoved his gloved hands against the glass, lifting them. He could feel the slick surface, even beneath his thin gloves. He'd always had very sensitive fingers. No callouses—he'd never worked as a laborer a day in his life.

A faint trail of dust descended around the window now that he'd opened it. He massaged at his neck, wincing against a crick.

He was moving at a quick pace now. Three dead already. Two in one this time. But slowing down wasn't an option. He had plans, big plans for the others. He was only just getting started.

He closed his eyes for a moment, inhaling deeply through his nostrils. Then, he slipped through the window, landing inside the bathroom, and rolling his shoulders.

He was in.

And no one had seen him. No one had heard him.

This was *his* superpower of course. Characters of all sorts existed in the pages of stories. They always had some gift, some ability. His mother, the witch, had locked him upstairs. No one had heard him scream. No one had seen him suffer.

It didn't matter what time of day—he'd been avoided, ignored.

He'd once, even, thought he was invisible.

Now, he knew better.

He was simply undetectable. Unseen, unheard, unnoticed, a culmination of all things neglectful. For his chosen life of work, of enjoyment, this was an immense gift.

He waited a moment, standing in the bathroom and listening for the voices on the other side of the door. He could still hear the faint prattle of Gretel speaking on her phone. But Hansel wasn't speaking. He'd seen the large jock arrive, of course. But the young fellow often retired to his room for a session in front of his computer on some of the more objectionable websites.

People in this generation simply didn't read enough. Then again, he knew Hansel and Gretel. Knew how their story ended. He didn't know what it might feel to discover a candy house in the woods... His little book of prophecies, the stories he knew beforehand, gave him ample time to change the ending.

He tutted to himself, and pushed the bathroom door open, allowing it to swing into the hall. He glanced at the mirror on the door, using it to watch the living room. Gretel was still moving, gesticulating wildly with one hand, her brown curls bouncing. She hadn't noticed the motion.

He'd go after Hansel first. The real threat.

He wet his lips briefly, grinning now, sensing the familiar rush of adrenaline as excitement bruited through his blood stream. Then, he stepped into the hall.

No screams. No shouts. As luck would have it, Gretel was facing the complete wrong direction. Neglected, ignored, unnoticed. Just like always. He didn't crouch, didn't tiptoe, just strode confidently down the hall in the direction of the bedrooms.

He reached the brother's door. A sign on it read *Warning. Toxic Waste.* He grinned at the sign. At least the fellow was self-aware. He was toxic and a waste of space. All of them were. No happy endings for this home.

He twisted the door handle and pushed into the room.

The big guy was sitting in an equally large desk chair, facing a computer with a comforter over his waist, his eyes glazed, his hand near his belt. Figures were performing unmentionable acts on the screen.

Again, Hansel was too enamored with his pictures, too distracted by the thick earphones on his head, he didn't look back. Didn't even notice the arrival of his fate.

The man paused, glancing around the room, noticing a stack of comic books and a couple of posters of comic book characters above the bed. He paused next to the closet door, behind the seated twin. The man's stinky football kit lay on the ground. Toxic waste indeed. The helmet sat on top of the discarded clothing.

The man bent over, picked up the helmet, hefted it.

Only then, did Hansel realize someone was in his room.

"Shit," he snapped, turning sharply, and looking over his shoulder. His hand moved quickly too, both, in fact. One clicking the computer screen off, the other rising to his chest as if he'd simply been scratching an itch. “Penelope, you rat! I told you to knock before—”

He went quiet suddenly, eyes bugging as he stared at the strange man in his bedroom.

This, even more than the pain, was *his* favorite part. He could smell the fear. The confusion, then a decision towards terror. He wiggled his gloved fingers.

“Hello,” he said in a conversational tone. “How are you?”

“Do—do I know you?” the large teenager asked, his voice deep, but also cracking at times.

“No, no, not yet. I'm going to spend some time with you and your sister, though. I'm going to hurt both of you.”

The big man's eyes bugged. He sneered in a casual sort of way as if reacting to a poorly timed joke from a friend. “You Penny's friend?” he asked.

The man frowned at the thick-headed youth. Sometimes, words just didn't work. So, he hefted the helmet and tested just how thick that skull really was. He slammed the metal into the side of Hansel's skull. Once, twice. Blood flecked the computer screen. A third blow, and Hansel didn't even have time to react, to shout—nothing.

Now, he just lay slumped, half sprawled over his chair, bleeding from his forehead.

The man stood there, panting from the quick exertion, still holding the helmet. His muscles twitched, strained beneath his clothing.

That's when he heard the sharp intake of breath. The sudden pause, then the scream.

He turned slowly, in no desire to rush any of this. Gretel was standing in the door, her phone no longer in hand suggesting she'd ended the call already. But her brown eyes in her dark, smooth skin were the size of quarters. Her mouth hung open, and she just stared at the man in her brother's bedroom.

“Hello Gretel,” he murmured, nodding politely at her. He pointed at her brother. “You're next.”

She just stared at him, gaping, then spun on her heel, reacting quicker than her brother had, but with far more fear. She sprinted down the hall, towards the front door.

He gave her a second to take the lead. He liked it when they ran.

“Ready or not,” he called down the hall, his voice echoing. “Here I come!”

Then, bloody football helmet still clutched in one hand, he also broke into a sprint, grinning so widely, he thought he must look like a jack-o-lantern.

CHAPTER NINETEEN

Ilse stepped back into the room in the hotel where Mr. Clement was speaking animatedly with his lawyer. The moment she entered the room, though, the woman frowned, holding up a shushing finger until Clement went silent, and then pointing that same finger towards Ilse's face. “You can't be in here,” she snapped angrily.

Ilse didn't retreat, however, remaining standing in the doorway. She didn't step forward, either, however, preferring not to confront the woman by trespassing a perceived physical boundary. Instead, in as docile a tone as she could manage, she said, “I'd like to speak with your client.”

“You've already been speaking with him,” the woman snapped back. “Don't think we won't be filing a complaint.”

Ilse ignored the lawyer now, looking towards Clement. “It doesn't look good for you. I know you know that.”

He just glared at her, like a child hiding behind the legs of a mother. The lawyer began to speak again, but Ilse now stepped fully into the room, allowing the door to swing shut behind her. She kept her tone even, calm, “I'm not disgusted by you,” she said, pointing towards the man.

This, only in part, was true. She could find the disgust if she looked close enough. But also, Ilse knew how to *choose* her emotions. She didn't get this far with her clients by picking them apart for the revolting thoughts or acts they performed due to their own pain. Pain beget pain. Sawyer had his own way of handling things. She was grateful for protectors like him who put men like this behind bars.

But that wasn't her role. She'd always known how to find mercy for even the most depraved sorts.

Then again... could she say the same for her father? Her stepmother... She suppressed this unnerving though, her stomach twisting.

The man looked stunned at her words, staring at her.

“My disgust won't help you,” Ilse said simply. “It won't help anyone now. You're here, you're going to go to prison most likely. I am sorry that you will suffer because of your choices.” She chose her words carefully, calmly. She didn't want to lie, but she also knew that sometimes one caught more bees with honey. And also... she knew her own heart and mind too much to live in constant judgment, even of depravity and perversion.

She had her own demons, her own fears, her own irrational and intrusive thoughts. Sometimes, she wondered if she was the one, like her sister Heidi, who deserved to be behind bars. Heidi, though, was dead now. Ilse lived.

Life was hardly fair.

"My disgust won't help," she said, "But I will try to. I need your cooperation to do that," she said simply.

The man stared at her. The lawyer was scowling. "It's a trick," the woman snapped. "Don't listen—"

Ilse kept going. "I'm not going to tell you off. I'm not going to try and leverage your clear sense of shame. You need help, sir. I know that and you know that. I'm willing to help you."

Clement just watched her now, breathing slow, shallow puffs. He blinked and swallowed, then murmured, "Help me? You can speak to the DA, yes? You can set me free..."

Ilse shook her head. "That's not how I can help. But I'm a clinical therapist. I know people who work in the prison systems. Good people. People who don't judge. Merciful people. You have a choice before you now, sir. Life may or may not have been hard on you. But if you are willing to try, you don't have to waste the next few years of your life. The bars on your cell might very well be the best thing to ever happen to you." She shrugged. "If you do the work, if you allow others in, if you're willing to try, you can get the help you need. You can come out the other side of this experience whole rather than broken. Do you understand me?"

The lawyer was just staring at her now as if Ilse were loony tunes. She didn't want to think what Sawyer might have said at this gentler approach. To Sawyer, this man was nothing more than a scumbag. A man who feasted his eyes on the abuse of defenseless, young children.

Ilse herself had suffered as a child. Her sisters, her brothers. She knew firsthand what it was to be subjected to predators without intervention.

But she also knew that in every human there was the potential for healing.

She never would have become a trauma counselor if that wasn't the case. She lived her life on this very hope. More often than not, she'd been disappointed. But the times when she wasn't were worth the risk of hoping.

Besides... another part of her was just sick of it. She'd seen a man behind prison bars back in Germany. He hadn't seemed the same at first, but then the same monster from before had emerged in her gaze.

She traced her fingers along the looping tattoo over her wrist. *Take captive every thought...*

For one strange moment, standing in that office room on the second floor of the hotel, Ilse felt tears coming to her eyes. She thought of all the pain her father had caused. Of all the pain men like Clement fed on. Who did that? Who enjoyed the suffering of children?

But she also knew suffering only beget suffering. Revenge led to revenge. Mercy... mercy was the harder road. The more dangerous choice. Ilse wasn't Sawyer, wasn't the law, wasn't the many nagging, incessant voices that might excoriate a broken man like Clement. Like any of the others they'd tracked and caught.

"You'd do that?" Clement said softly, staring at her.

"Look," the lawyer began, "Don't speak, this is just—"

But he interjected, cutting her off, "Hang on, look," he said quickly, staring at Ilse now and completely ignoring his lawyer, "I'm not proud of what I've done. I—I know you'll find that stuff on the hard drive. I don't know how you knew what was there... but... but well...," he stared at the table, his head hanging, tears in his eyes now.

To her stunned surprise, Ilse found something close to pity rising in her chest.

"The fairy tales," she murmured, "Staying on track. We have a killer reenacting them. I'm not an expert, sir, but you are. Can you help me?"

He looked her dead in the eyes. "If I do, will you help me?"

She returned the look, paused, considering this. "Either way," she said at last, "I'll help you. It's not an exchange, it's an offer followed by a request."

The lawyer was still glaring, shaking her head in derision at it all, but Clement massaged his knuckles, his handcuffs shifting on the table. Then, he said, carefully, "People obsessed with fairy tales, like myself are often chasing the notion of a happy ending. We never had one before. We don't often think they can be found in reality..."

"So it's a form of wish fulfillment?"

"I mean, yes. What isn't? Everyone dabbles in escapism. But... but some of us," he swallowed, "we liken the villains in the stories to the villains in our own lives." His eyes flashed with barely concealed hatred, his lips tightening. It took him a moment to move on from whatever emotion had suddenly arisen, but then, when he did, he continued, "We see ourselves as the protagonists. We believe we're suffering trials necessary to reach our own happily ever after. Do you understand? I didn't kill anyone. I swear it. But if the person you're looking for is somehow involved in our scene... They don't believe in happy endings. They're not one of us. See? If they were, they wouldn't try to ruin the lives of others. We can be vain, conceited, whatever... Like everyone," Clement said, his sweaty brow bobbing as he moved with the motion of his own words. "But we're not killers. I...," he trailed off, frowning. "Actually... I can think of a man. Someone who, well, who often reviewed my books." He frowned again.

"Someone who reviewed your books?"

"Yes. He hated them," Mr. Clement said. "Didn't like the horror elements. But if you read my stories closely there *are* happy endings. For the villains. Villains are people too, aren't they?" He said, a hopeful lilt to his words.

Ilse didn't respond, instead nodding once and saying, "This reviewer, you think he might provide some insight?"

Clement snorted, shaking his head. "He hated my books. Passionately. I looked him up once, actually. Wasn't hard. When you search my name, his results come up on the first page." Clement sneered at this. "He runs a blog, self-publishing essays that dissect fairy tales as cautionary tales in the modern world. He's not creative. He's a critical hack. But he hated my work. Not because he doesn't like happy endings, but because he *hates* villains. See?"

"I'm not sure I do."

Clement leaned forward now, shrugging off the hand of his lawyer pressing to his arm. "He didn't think villains deserved happy endings. He thought they should be killed. Like the dogs they are. That's the phrase he used. He called us—er, *them,* dogs. If you want someone who'd kill for fairy tales, you should find this professor.

"Online, he goes by the handle LongshotPHD."

"Can you spell that for me?" Ilse said.

As he did, she nodded slowly, cataloging the response. She'd have to borrow a laptop or one of the officers' smartphones to search for the name and the reviews. But at least it was some type of lead. One way or another, it would provide some level of insight into the psyche of such men.

“Thank you,” Ilse said once Clement had finished. She began to turn, but he cleared his throat, raising his cuffed hands hesitantly.

She glanced back.

“That... that help you promised,” he said slowly. “If—if I do go away,” his voice strained with panic, his eyes wide, “You'll still help me, yes? I—I know I shouldn't have... I know I didn't... I... I just...”

Ilse looked him dead in the eyes. “I promise to help. I'll set you up with a reputable counselor. You have to want to change sir. That's where we all start. It's where I started. It's where all my clients do. It's not a badge of shame but of courage.” She nodded once more, taking a pause to feel an odd, dawning sense of satisfaction. Somehow, this was more satisfying than any of the arrests she'd made so far. It felt like the times she spoke with her clients. Helping them. Then again, putting predators behind bars *did* help people, didn't it?

She paused, considering this. Just because someone was arrested didn't mean they stopped being human. Perhaps that was what she was missing with her father. Perhaps she was seeing him like a monster rather than a wounded person.

But how did that help? What, if anything, did that mean?

She gave a brief nod towards the lawyer, then to Clement, then she turned, pushing through the door and stepping into the hall. She looked towards the nearest officer by the door and cleared her throat. “Excuse me, but I need to borrow your phone to look something up. It's important.”

CHAPTER TWENTY

Ilse was standing outside the hotel now. Sawyer, thankfully, was still there, sitting in an idling car with the windows down and the sunroof open, even though night had fallen. In the darkness, he looked a gloomy silhouette outlined through the faintly tinted windows of the loaner sedan.

She stood on the curb, watching the car but not approaching it as she waited for her phone to connect. She lowered the phone, double-checking the number to make sure she'd recorded it correctly from the website she'd found on the cop's phone, then lifted her device again, waiting.

Her dumb flip phone often had spotty connections, even in the city, but thankfully, after another long ring, there came a silence, then a breath and a voice, “Admissions office—how can I help you?”

“Umm, hello,” Ilse said cautiously. “I'm calling to speak with Professor Seatman. Is he in?”

“I'm sorry,” the voice said. “Who is this?”

“My name is Agent Beck,” Ilse said, flinching at the introduction. Normally, she would let Sawyer bandy about the term “agent.” But now, she knew she needed an inroad. Still, the word didn't quite fit her name or her lips. “I'm with the FBI,” she pressed on. “We need to speak with Mr. Seatman right away.”

Indeed, the reviews on Mr. Clement's books posted by the professor had paled in comparison to some of his blog postings. The call for violence against anyone who might be deemed a villain—even given the 'fairy tale' context—had immediately caught Ilse's attention. She thought of their last victim, Jackson, the farmer. He'd tried to start a new life after an assault in his younger years. Perhaps in Seatman's mind, or one of his blog reader's minds, Mr. Jackson was the sort of villain that didn't *deserve* a happy ending.

“Umm,” the voice on the other line lost some of its professionalism. “Do you mind telling us what this is about?”

Us. Someone else was in the room. A supervisor? The professor himself?

“I'm afraid I'm not at liberty to divulge that,” Ilse replied. “Can you transfer me to the professor's number, please?"

"I'm afraid I can't do that."

Ilse frowned. "Why not?"

"It's school policy, but look, that doesn't matter. Professor Seatman isn't here."

"Oh? You mean he's already left for the night." Ilse glanced at her phone, lifting it from her face. It was nearly 7:30 PM. Daylight had retreated. Professors were notorious for long hours, and the school admissions' office hours went until eight according to their website.

"No," the voice returned. "It's just, Mr. Seatman has taken a leave of absence."

"How long?" she said, feeling a prickle along her back.

"Just these last few days... Umm, let me check... It started..." A pause, the sound of a keyboard, then more confidently, "Last week Tuesday."

Ilse blinked. "So nearly eight days?" That would have been before the murders started. What were the odds? "Did he give a reason for the leave of absence."

The voice paused on the other end. Ilse heard a murmured exchange with someone else in the room. "My supervisor says that's confidential," the voice replied.

Ilse paused for a moment, considering her next move. Mercy was all well and good, but she wasn't a one trick pony either. She considered how Sawyer might approach this particular problem, then settled quickly on a solution. "I see. I suppose we'll just have to send agents to the school then, to go through your files and confiscate computers. We should have the warrant by midnight, maybe early morning. Try not to go to sleep, we don't want to have to wake the president at his home. What's your name again, miss? Just so we can tell him who we were speaking to? Your supervisor's name too, please."

Another pause, a faint breath, then the sound of fumbling and a new voice replied. "I'm the coordinator of admissions affairs," the new voice said, sounding flustered. "It's not a big deal, really. There's no need for any of that."

"We need answers," Ilse replied sternly.

"We don't know you're FBI," the voice returned.

"I'm texting you a photo of my ID now," Ilse said. She already stored a photo on her dumb phone. The camera was quite grainy. But after pressing send, Ilse waited only a moment, before the voice sighed. "Agent Beck?"

"Yes."

"Right, well, look, it's not a big deal. Professor Seatman had a bit of a... hmm, shall we call it *episode* in class last week. For his sake he's taking a bit of a break."

"What sort of episode?" Ilse said, unrelenting like a hound with a bone.

"It was... was mostly nothing," the voice insisted. "Just—Look, Seatman received comments from some of his students online."

"On his blog?"

"Y-yes, you know about that? What's this about?"

"Focus, please," Ilse said. "What sort of comments."

The faculty member snorted but tried to cover the derisive sound with a cough. "Mr. Seatman received some critiques from anonymous upper classmen about a few of his articles online. He didn't take it particularly well."

The first voice, the secretary's called out, "He started yelling at us in class. Threatened to fail us all!"

Ilse blinked in surprise. She felt a faint jolt of bleak humor at the irony. Mr. Seatman had left strongly worded, harsh criticism online of any book or fairy tale he didn't like. He never pulled his punches. It seemed fitting that such a judgmental man had a breakdown after receiving some criticism of his own.

So it often was with such people.

"Thank you," Ilse said. "Can you tell me where I might find Mr. Seatman, please? I need an address."

***

Ilse noted how quiet Sawyer was on the drive over, not that this was news. He was often quiet. But when Ilse had mentioned the source of the new lead, and the lead itself, he'd only looked beleaguered. Now, he just drove down the quiet suburban streets in the western part of the city.

Ilse didn't try to draw him into conversation now. It wasn't her business to settle whatever demons Sawyer was battling in his own mind. He was a tough man, a willful man, unrelenting. She'd seen him covered in sweat, slicked with mud, marching through rough, forested terrain for hours and hours without lagging. She'd seen him, at the end of such effort, climb into a killer's lair without an ounce of fear. She'd seen this same man, in his free time, patrol misty mountain paths in search for another killer, his eyes fixed on the side of the road, his sheer stubbornness holding exhaustion at bay.

Now, that same stubbornness that conquered physical lack was out to play, and it was directed at Ilse. She still wasn't entirely sure what she'd done to earn his distrust, but this couldn't be solved in the middle of an urgent case.

As they pulled to a slow, grinding halt in the driveway of a large, four thousand square foot plus home, Ilse's attention diverted to the crimson facade. Beyond the house, she spotted a large, complex redwood patio with an intricate set of sloping stairs. The edge of a covered pool was also visible next to a shared tennis court.

“Guess it pays to teach after all,” Ilse murmured beneath her breath. She looked at Sawyer. “Are you coming?”

In response, he turned off the engine, and pushed out of the car onto the drive, stretching his lanky legs.

Grateful for the backup, but not waiting to make a big deal out of it lest she spook Sawyer back into the car, Ilse moved along the drive of the large home. It wasn't quite a mansion, but it aspired to be one.

Under the night, the orange glow from the house looked as if it were preparing for a real estate photograph. Ilse heard faint music coming from within the home, the sound of strings and piano twittering on the air.

The front door, she realized as they drew near, was open.

She frowned, her hand slowly moving to her holster. Sawyer had tensed now too. He nodded down, and Ilse spotted the shoe which lay discarded, and upside down, just within the door.

“Hello there,” she murmured faintly.

She eased the door open and spotted a second shoe—this one also discarded, but somehow had landed *on top* of an aquarium sitting on a small table by the front door.

The shoes weren't the only haphazardly discarded clothing items. A jacket was sitting in the middle of the carpet, and sweatpants were bunched up next to those, leading a trail of fabric towards an adjoining room.

“Hello!” Ilse called into the house. “FBI! Geoff Seatman, are you in?”

The music from the other room had reached a crescendo of strings and percussive. Ilse waited for the sound to fade before calling again. “Mr. Seatman! Professor? Are you home? This is the FBI!”

She heard, over the swell of music, a groan and faint response from the other room. Her pulse quickened and she took hurried steps down the hall, away from the already open door.

She came to a halt facing a study and frowned.

A man was laying on a leather couch, a scale replica of a battle frigate on the table above him, like some sort of museum ornament. Paintings on the walls displayed scenes from fairy tales. Ilse recognized pixies with wings, big toothy wolves, and an impressionistic portrait with jarring colors of a grizzly bear.

The man on the couch was half naked, wearing only his boxers. He had a glass bottle squeezed against his chest so tight, it pressed into the skin like dough over a bread pan. Other bottles littered the wooden floor around the man.

"Mr. Seatman?" Ilse asked, frowning. "Hello, sir, are you alright?"

The man blinked a few times, propping his head up. He had long, white hair that hadn't been trimmed in years. He wore a wild goatee, also white, but his eyebrows were as black as soot. He had blue eyes like winter seas, but the effect was somewhat ruined by the way they were half hooded, puffy and red, fluttering every couple of seconds.

"Gre—shh—janish? Hi Janish!" he slurred happily. "Welcome to the shloshy fiber."

Ilse blinked, unable to interpret the drunken spiel.

"Mr. Seatman," she said slowly, "Are you alright sir?"

He just wagged his white beard at her, and took another sip form the bottle on his chest. A red mark stained his skin where he'd been pressing the bottle.

"Sir," Sawyer interjected, more sternly, "We need you to get to your feet."

The distinguished professor raised a hand and flashed the bird, gyrating his hips in a clear gesture intended to offend.

Sawyer frowned, taking a step into the study. "Get up," Sawyer said.

Ilse, wincing, sidled past her partner, stepping near the man who smelled of beer burps and stale sweat. "Hey, professor," she said, doing her best to inhale through her mouth, "we need to speak with you about some of the items you've posted online."

"Who are you?" he asked, blinking and staring at her as if seeing her for the first time.

"My name is Doctor Beck," Ilse said, only a second later realizing she'd dropped off the word agent. Perhaps a man like this, involved in academics, might respect a shared education pattern.

He burped in her face, sitting up now, and waving his beer bottle around like a king's scepter.

Ilse scowled. "Professor, I need you to sit up now, please."

The man looked her in the eye, or, at least, tried to, but his gaze kept shifting, his red-ringed pupils widening. He hiccupped and then said. "Hello, darling..."

She reached out to try and guide him to his feet. This man didn't seem like a cold-blooded killer. But as her hand landed on his arm, he scowled at her fingers. Then, he swiped at her with his bottle, trying to dislodge her grip.

It was an easy enough blow to dodge, and she did so, withdrawing her hand, but at the same time, Sawyer moved in with a furious shout. As the beer bottle swished harmlessly past, Sawyer's hand shot out, grabbing the man by the collar and shoving him back onto the couch.

The man yelled but Sawyer placed himself between Ilse and the bottle-throwing fellow, his shoulders trembling with rage.

"It's fine!" Ilse protested. "Sawyer, I'm fine. He didn't hit me."

Tom glanced at her, his eyes shining with some hidden fury. His teeth were set, and again, Ilse was reminded how Sawyer hadn't been acting like himself recently.

He kicked the glass bottle skittering across the ground and out of reach.

Ilse winced, touching Sawyer's shoulder which was still trembling; he began breathing heavily, holding the man by the collar against the couch, hissing a threatening sound beneath his breath. "Don't throw bottles," he said, his chill tone and words hardly matching his fiery demeanor.

The professor was groaning now, muttering, "I think I'm going to puke."

Sawyer, though, clicked his fingers, reaching for Ilse's handcuffs. Reluctantly, with a sigh, she said, "I'm fine, Tom. I'm more than fine."

He took the handcuffs and began to restrain the guy without so much as a word.

CHAPTER TWENTY ONE

Ilse and Sawyer led the professor out of his quasi-mansion, towards where a police cruiser was pulling up next to the curb, lights flashing. Ilse heard Sawyer whistle, and he waved over one of the cops who hurried out of the vehicle and jogged over, panting as he arrived.

"Take him to the drunk tank," Sawyer said, giving the inebriated professor a little push on the shoulder. The cop nodded, grabbed the man and began leading him back towards the car. As he did, Sawyer turned, rubbing at the back of his head and staring towards the house.

Ilse watched him out of the corner of her eye. Once he'd calmed a bit, and the back of the police car slammed shut again, she murmured, beneath her breath, "That was an overreaction."

Sawyer looked at her, then looked away. The two of them stood on the path leading up to the front door of the house. The red and blue lights from the police car behind them reflected off the windows. Ilse knew it wasn't on her to psychoanalyze coworkers, but on the other hand, Sawyer was clearly hurting. He'd restrained himself in handling the inebriated suspect, but she'd rarely seen him so angry. In addition, things could easily get out of hand if she didn't say something. He'd shattered a window. He'd been on the verge of striking a drunk suspect.

Ilse kept her tone calm but continued pressing. "You know it was."

"He tried to strike you with a weapon," Sawyer countered. "I did what I had to."

Ilse shook her head. "No. If you really thought that, you'd be angrier. You'd wonder why I was telling you off for coming to my defense. But since you're not, it means you know it was an overreaction. Sawyer, please, I'm not trying to frustrate you, but I need to know what's going on. Are you okay?"

He turned to look at her now, standing on the driveway. The sound of the police radio chatter could be heard on the air from the open front door of the cruiser. The two cops were checking their suspect in the back seat. One of the cops called, "He okay, or does he need medical?"

Sawyer retorted, "He's fine! Take him to a holding cell. We'll be there when he sobers up."

A new voice snorted at this comment, and a figure sitting on the porch next door made a tisking sound with their tongue. "Good luck on that," the neighbor called.

Ilse and Sawyer turned, looking towards this new figure who was leaning on the railing and watching them both. The man was young and had a glass of wine in one hand and a quizzical expression on his face. He looked like a banker, or a lawyer perhaps, with good looks and intelligence behind those eyes.

He waved towards the two agents. Ilse, bemused, waved back.

Sawyer looked off in disgust.

"You live there?" Ilse called, pointing towards the second house.

"Last I checked," he said. "Mr. Seatman there isn't sobering any time soon."

"So you said. Why's that?"

The man on the porch sniffed and took another faint sip of his wine before placing it back on the rail. "Because he's been in there for nearly a week, playing that horrible music. The only people who come or leave are the grocery delivery drivers who drop off his thinly disguised bottles. They've been coming in and out for days now." The man on the porch shrugged then glanced back towards the police car.

"Is everything alright? He didn't do anything stupid, did he?"

Ilse rubbed at her chin, but then just shook her head. "We don't know yet." She nodded again in gratitude towards the neighbor but turned promptly away, presenting him with her back and facing Sawyer again. In a quieter tone, she said, "What do you think, Tom?"

He looked at her. "This was your angle, Beck. I just followed the call."

"You bludgeoned the call. But point taken." Ilse crossed her arms, looking towards the miserable form of the professor in the back seat of the police cruiser.

Her mind was racing now—she could deal with Sawyer's attitude issues later. For now, she had a murderer to catch. And by the looks of things, corroborated by the testimony of the neighbor, professor Seatman hardly fit the bill.

They couldn't question him now, either, as they would have to wait for him to sober up in a holding cell before interrogation. But if the neighbor was right, and Seatman had been on a week-long bender, shut-in, then he certainly hadn't been out murdering folk. The crimes took a far more alert mind and nimble physicality.

Besides, in his current state, he didn't seem like the sort who had the type of discipline and determination to pull off these murders. This wasn't a bold man striking in broad daylight—this was a wounded child nursing their hurt feelings with bottle after bottle. When he'd tried to strike her, he'd missed completely. Then, when Sawyer had manhandled him, he'd gone down with ease.

Did she really believe this fellow had anything to do with the murders? Unless he was simply faking... But she pictured the house, the smell of the guy, how atrophied he looked... It wasn't an act.

She frowned again towards the back of the police cruiser, feeling a dawning sense of frustration rising within her.

It didn't fit.

It wasn't him, was it?

They could make sure once they questioned him, but even that would have to wait. But waiting was the one thing they couldn't afford to do. They simply didn't have the time.

She bit her lip in frustration, scowling.

"You good?" Sawyer said, watching her, his tone a bit gentler now that the topic of conversation had shifted from him.

She scowled back. "I'm going to have to cancel appointments tomorrow," she said.

"With your clients? Why?"

"Because if we don't get a handle on this case, we're going to lose others. I... I'm sure I'm right, Tom. The connection is fairy tales."

"I mean—you hear how it sounds though, right?"

"I hear it," she retorted. "But I'm convinced."

"So...," he trailed off and shrugged. "What do you want to do about it?"

"First," she said, "I want you to tell me what's wrong. Why are you acting this way?"

"Doc, drop it. Cancel, those appointments if you want, but that doesn't mean you get to do a number on me. I'm fine."

She hissed in frustration, jamming her hands in her pocket and feeling her own nerves rising. She didn't want to drop it. Normally, she was measured in her approach with clients and colleagues alike. But now, she could feel her temper rising. Perhaps from the lack of sleep the night before, or perhaps simply from Sawyer's stubborn streak which ran as deep as the furrow on his brow when glaring at Mr. Seatman.

"Fine. It's gone," Ilse said. "Now you let it go too. I need your help, Tom." Before he could reply, she turned on her heel, marching back towards the house.

Normally, the locals were the ones tasked with searching a suspect's residence, but she needed something to do with her hands. Needed another lead, somewhere to turn.

So she marched straight back to the large home, eyes narrowed. She knew immediately where she would start the search. In the same, odoriferous place they'd found Mr. Seatman's half-conscious form.

CHAPTER TWENTY TWO

The large, scale-size frigate was slightly tilted when Ilse returned into the study. Her foot struck a glass bottle, sending it rolling across the floor. She inhaled slowly through her mouth, and yet could still detect the faintest odors lingering on the air. She waved a hand beneath her nose, standing with her back to the door. Behind her, she could sense Sawyer still lingering outside the house. She didn't particularly care if he was watching her or not.

She knew, now, she would have to cancel the mornings appointments with her clients—something she was loathe to do. Those people needed her, and by canceling it felt like she was letting them down.

Still, others needed her too—namely the victims of this newest serial killer. Sometimes, the sheer state of humanity seemed an insurmountable object. But now, she was faced with a different type of mess.

This one coming in the variety of glass bottles, empty food wrappers, and what looked like a discarded pair of pants beneath one of the windows.

The place was a mess. On the desk, in an overflowing wastepaper basket, she spotted more than one manuscript jammed into the tiny, metal container. Shredded paper, like confetti, littered the desk as well.

Ilse inhaled shakily, scanning the area while wearing the severest of frowns. There was nothing to find here, was there? A navel-gazing professor had gone on a bender, set off by online criticism of his own critiques. This wasn't their killer—surely not...

Even when they had a chance to interview the man, she wasn't sure they'd find much of anything.

She tapped a finger against her lips as she moved around the edge of the desk and peered into the wastepaper basket. The title of the jammed manuscript simply read, *Untitled, a treatise of allegory in childhood stories.*

She resisted the urge to roll her eyes as she moved away from the desk, stepping over a yet untouched sixpack beneath the desk chair.

A small bookshelf by the window carried a modest collection of books with old-fashioned, curved binding. Some of them leather, others flimsy, cardboard like material. Ilse frowned as she leaned in, studying some of the books. She felt a faint breeze suddenly coming from behind her, and she turned to spot a small desk fan hidden beneath the large model frigate. The air current from the fan ruffled some of the shredded strands of paper draped over the desks.

The man had exacted his violence externally on his *own* work. He'd taken the criticism from his students and gone on a bender. This was the sort of person who harmed themselves when hurt by others. Was he really the type to also go and exact vengeance in the form of murder?

It didn't seem to fit with his personality.

The more she came to know the professor, the less she suspected he was their culprit. With this also came a slow, gnawing sense of impending doom.

If the real killer was still out there, biding his time, then Ilse didn't even know where to start. She studied the desk, searching for... for insight into the mind of their suspect. One could learn a lot about a person by perusing their desk. She turned away from the desk again, but as she did, the small fan beneath the model frigate sent a few strands of shredded paper flying, skittering across the wood then tumbling over the edge of the furniture piece.

She scowled, turning off the fan and moving it to glance at a notepad beneath it. The paper was blank. She moved on to one of the drawers, opening it to find a stack of bills. She glanced towards a filing cabinet, but the drawers were locked. She turned, kicking a couple of the ripped strands of paper, and frowning at more curls of ripped parchment on the table. She leaned in, brushing the paper aside.

She began to lift one of the strands of parchment, but then stopped, looking on the desk. A book lay hidden beneath the ripped paper.

A book lying open.

She stepped over the sixpack once more, avoiding a gas-station sandwich wrapper on the floor, and reached out delicately towards the open book. She brushed some of the shredded paper off to the side as if it were strands of limp pasta. She slowly closed the book and frowned at the title.

Roget's Collection of Fairy Tales.

She opened the book, scanning the table of contents, her brow still low. And that's when she spotted the titles of the stories.

On page four The Gingerbread Man. Page twelve had The Ugly Duckling. Following, on page thirty came the story of Jack and the

Beanstalk...

She felt a faint shiver down her back as she double-checked the order.

The same order the killer was using. First the marathon runner, then the fashion model, then the bean farmer. One after the other. She also knew, from her experience researching different collections online, that most weren't in this particular order. Which meant...

Meant what?

She frowned. Professor Seatman wasn't the killer, of that she was nearly certain. But whoever the killer was, he seemed to be following a preordained plan. Or, perhaps, a table of contents. She tapped a finger against the next story on the list, beneath Jack and the Beanstalk.

Hansel and Gretel.

"What are the odds?" she murmured to herself, shaking her head. It was the same order, the exact same order. She knew what Sawyer would think. But she'd combed through twenty collections online—none of them were in this order. Well, one had been the same order, but the stories had been midway through the tome.

This book started that way and also... She stared at the cover. An old, leatherbound thing. She flipped to the publishing page.

1972. An old book.

Old enough for the killer to have possessed as a child? Clearly there was some emotional stunting involved in all of this. If the fairy tale theory was real, and she felt certain it was, then the killer must have had the same or similar edition.

And if that was the case...

She moved back to the Table of Contents, heart pounding.

Hansel and Gretel.

Then they also had a lead.

"Tom!" she called out over her shoulder, her voice excited. "Tom!" she yelled louder. She frowned when she received no response and turned, moving back towards the hall. She came to a stop, spotting Sawyer standing in the entryway, frowning at a stack of receipts by the front door.

"Tom," she said, her voice inquisitive now.

He looked at her, then pointed to the receipts. "Bastard has been ordering food all week."

She winced, nodding slowly.

"He's been shut in," Sawyer said, scowling. He rubbed his jaw, looking up. "Not gonna matter if he sobers, Ilse. It ain't him."

"Forget about him," she said hurriedly. "Look what I found." She held up the tome of fairy tales, wagging it in Sawyer's direction.

"A book?"

"A book of fairy tales. No, no don't do that with your mouth."

"I'm not doing anything."

"That's your disapproving look. Yes—that. When you press your lips like that. Hear me out, Tom. It's the same order. Look—No, here, take it. Look!"

Sawyer reluctantly accepted the extended tome, allowing Ilse to guide him to the table of contents. He gave a faint huff and shrugged. "Alright," he muttered. "Looking. What exactly should I be looking *at*?"

Ilse tapped the story titles. "Look at the first one."

Sawyer did and shrugged.

"The second," she said.

His shrug turned to a grunt.

By the third tap and point he was frowning. He pulled the book a bit closer, lifting it as if to read it more clearly.

"See!" she said excitedly.

"Could be a coincidence," Sawyer said.

"Or maybe not," she countered. "And if I'm right, look at the fourth entry."

He did. "Hansel and Gretel, yeah?"

"It's pronounced *gre*-tel. Like in the word gray. Not like greet."

"Whatever, Gre-tel."

She stared at Sawyer for a moment, wrinkling her nose. "Don't you know the story?"

He scowled back at her. "So what," he said. "I was busy mucking stalls and rising at dawn. Didn't have time for fairy tales as a kid. Sue me."

Ilse shook her head, trying not to roll her eyes. That comment alone was the most Sawyer-esque thing she'd heard all day. Of course he'd never read Hansel and Gretel. Of course he'd been mucking stalls at dawn. She tried to keep her exasperation hidden and instead, tone as gentle as she could manage, said, "Tom, Hansel and Gretel were twin kids. Two lost children in a wood that were kidnapped by a witch."

Now, Sawyer's irritation faded, and he sobered a bit. "You think he's going after kids next?"

"I—I don't know. That would be a strong deviation for him. Especially if he's acting out some childhood fantasy."

"So what, doc, we looking for twins?"

"I—I don't know. Maybe... we should look for missing kids in the last twenty-four hours. Might not be twins. Might just be siblings, or friends. Can we do that? He's escalating with the story component. The vines with the farmer were an added dramatic flair. Who knows what he's planning next?"

"Kids or siblings. On it," Sawyer said. Now that children were threatened, she saw the way his eyes narrowed, watched as he seemed to hit a new gear. Threatening kids was one of the main ways to get Sawyer back in the game.

But Ilse could feel her own concerns now. What if she was right? What if this killer was going after children?

She set her teeth, feeling a sense of horror and fury.

"We need those reports. Anything and anyone within two hours of Seattle."

"Any kids?"

"It would be *two,*" Ilse countered. "Two kids either related or friends. From the same area."

"Got it."

Sawyer's phone was already in his hand, and as he lifted the device, stalking back towards the front door, there was a renewed urgency in his step. Ilse followed after her partner, the initial excitement at the new lead now wearing off in the face of its obvious ramifications. As of yet, they hadn't taken a case with children involved...

She felt a lance of horror at the thought. Memories drifted back to her subconscious, threatening to rise to the surface of normally murky water.

She flinched, standing in the threshold of the doorway to the large home, closing her eyes and murmuring beneath her breath, "Two victims. Canadian. Air force. Assault. Narcissistic personality—"

But she was cut off as Sawyer said, "What the hell do you mean?" He paced back and forth on the patio, shaking his head. Ilse stepped back out into the night as well, watching her partner. Sawyer said, "That many? Just today? Any of them siblings? Twins?" He paused, frowning off into the night.

Ilse came closer and Sawyer switched his device to speaker. "Go on," he said, "Repeat what you told me, my partner's next to me."

A somewhat flustered voice on the other end of dispatch said, "W— there have been five new missing children reports in the last twelve hours alone. But none of them are siblings. I can go further back if you'd like. This week alone we're almost over a hundred—"

"Christ," Sawyer muttered beneath his breath.

Ilse rubbed at the tattoo circling her wrist, feeling her emotions threatening to withdraw. She reached out, patting Sawyer on the arm. She knew how he got when kids were threatened, but also, she had her own demons where that arena was concerned.

"Alright," Sawyer said, gritting his teeth and steadying himself. "Check back in two days. Any further and our guy would be breaking his apparent pattern."

A pause, some lingering, then, "Well... I had two sisters go missing but they were found at a friend's house. They'd just forgotten to call."

"Damn it, Jan, that's not what I mean," Sawyer said. "Anything still open?"

Another pause. Ilse noted these pauses were far longer than when they involved Rudiger. She supposed some people were simply better suited for sitting in front of machines for a living. The woman on the other end cleared her throat then said, "No siblings. No twins. No open cases of children taken from the same home or school within the last two days."

Sawyer grunted, lowering his phone and giving Ilse a long look. "Well?" he said.

Ilse just stood on the flagstone patio, shaking her head and frowning, trying to process what she was hearing. The number of inferred cases of missing children in Seattle alone was heartbreaking. She could still feel her emotions threatening to go into hiding. This was one of her many defense mechanisms when confronted with the underbelly of humanity.

She'd learned to hide at a very young age. If she numbed herself, she couldn't feel the pain, the humiliation, the shame and—most of all—the sheer horror.

But she was no longer a child. Her father was no longer tormenting her... at least, not up close and personal. For the sake of the case, she had to keep *all* parts of herself in the game. Emotions included.

"Alright," she said slowly. "So maybe we're wrong about this one. Kidnapping kids would get far too much attention. What if—"

Before she could continue, Sawyer's lowered phone, which he hadn't hung up, started squawking. A voice, it seemed, was raising its volume over the cheap speaker. Sawyer hesitated, then lifted the device. "What was that?" he said. "Repeat."

The voice on the other end seemed breathless but paused mid-sentence to start again. “I said we had 911 report for missing twins, but they're adults. Eighteen. I double-checked without the age restriction. A frantic mother called the operator.”

“Oh?” Ilse said, leaning towards the phone in Sawyer's hand. “What about?”

“She's reporting her two children missing,” the operator said hurriedly. “It didn't show up on the database because they're not children. They're both eighteen...”

“Both?” Ilse and Sawyer said at once.

“Twins,” the operator replied. “A boy and a girl who couldn't have been missing for more than three hours. Should I put her through?”

Ilse paused for a moment, considering this. “Was the mother on the scene when they were taken?”

“It—hang on.” The line went dead. Then it crackled back to life. “No, she wasn't; she tried calling, but her kids wouldn't answer. She drove by and saw a window open, the front door open. They were gone. But their car is still there.”

Ilse winced. “I see. Where is she now?”

“On the way to a police station, speaking on the phone.”

“Okay, in that case, no we don't need to speak with her yet. Just text us the address. Where were they taken from?”

Sawyer kept the phone aloft but was already moving rapidly back towards their vehicle. Ilse didn't hesitate to follow, her insides still swirling with that odd mixture of numbness and anticipation.

CHAPTER TWENTY THREE

Ilse slammed the door as she took the two steps from the street to the elevated sidewalk and scowled in the direction of the small townhouse centering the street. The left side of the duplex had police officers moving in and out. A woman wrapped in a shawl was sobbing next to a female officer who was trying to speak to the woman.

Ilse hesitated then scowled. “Thought they said the mother was on the way to the precinct,” she muttered.

Sawyer, at her side, just shrugged, shaking his head. He ignored the bawling woman and stepped right past, moving towards the front door. One of the cops recognized Sawyer and tipped his head in a greeting that Tom returned.

Ilse hesitated near the sobbing woman, wondering if she ought to comfort her. Sawyer though, gave an insistent tug on her arm, muttering beneath his breath, “Best thing you can do for her is find her kids. Come on.”

Ilse winced, but nodded, ducking her head, not making eye contact, then following Sawyer into the house.

Forensics seemed bunched at the end of a short hallway, three of them crowded in the doorway. Ilse glanced around the entrance. A single couch, a beanbag, and television sitting directly on the ground. The sort of room one might expect from college-aged kids. It was unusual for a brother and sister to live together, no doubt. But twins often played by different rules. She'd spent much of her life trying to *escape* her siblings, her family. She felt a strangely timed pang of jealousy at the idea of desiring to be around them.

“Bathroom?” she asked slowly.

Sawyer frowned, paused, then pointed towards a door centering the hall. “Tiled floor.”

The two of them moved towards this. Dispatch had mentioned an open bathroom window. Ilse paused in the doorway, staring across the blue and teal tiled floor, over a sink with a curling iron balanced precariously on the back of the tank. A giant mess of electrical cords hovered over the sink, far too close to any source of water than was advisable.

Ilse ignored the sink, though, frowning towards the window. It was ajar. It had been slid up.

She stepped towards the window, frowning and glancing into the alley.

"See anything?" Sawyer called from behind.

She just shook her head.

"I'll check the alley. You check the room."

She didn't speak but flashed a thumbs up, most of her attention still claimed by the open window. The killer had climbed through... had he known the window would be open? She peered at the small metal latching mechanism and felt a flicker of apprehension.

It was snapped. Someone had broken it.

It took some level of know-how to break a lock, didn't it? Did the killer have experience with breaking and entering?

She shook her head, cataloging this information for further use and then turning to move down the hall and side-step a forensic tech to now move in the direction of the room which drew most of law enforcement's attention.

She stepped past another figure, apologizing briefly, and sidled under a sign that read *Toxic Waste.* Then, peering into the room, she realized the source of their gathered attention. Blood stains on the carpet, and blood stains on a desk chair facing a computer screen. Ilse frowned towards a football helmet which had been left on the ground. She spotted a crimson stain containing strands of hair and felt a faint shiver up her spine.

She glanced towards the window beyond the computer desk, but this one was closed and looked as if it hadn't been tampered with. A couple of the forensic techs were dusting down the computer, and another was examining the blood stain on the carpet.

Ilse, though, was glancing towards a corkboard above the bed. On it, there were pictures of the twins and their families. Penny and Clyde Denzel were both good-looking, with bright smiles and eyes full of good humor.

Their parents were equally attractive, tall and athletic. There were other Polaroids of their friends on ski trips, surfing or pontooning on a lake.

Such a lively collection of memories, and now those same memories were threatened. Ilse looked to the two photos she recognized from the driver's license photos of Penny and Clyde. Both of them smiled out at the camera, their arms over each other's shoulders, though Clyde was a head and shoulders taller than his sister, so he was stooping a bit in the photo. They both had blonde hair and turtleneck sweaters in the image.

Ilse frowned suddenly, staring at the photos. Her gaze flickered along the corkboard, searching out the other photographs of the twins.

In each one, she spotted the same thing.

"Sawyer!" she called over her shoulder. "Tom, get in here!"

She dropped slowly to a knee, frowning at the item on the ground, careful not to step in the blood stain. She heard the sound of footsteps, jostling then a voice behind her. "You called?"

"Look at this," she said faintly.

Something brushed against her shoulder as Sawyer stooped next to her, following her indicated finger. "Yeah," he said. "Hair fiber."

"Yes," Ilse replied, "but—"

"Ah shit," Sawyer replied suddenly as realization struck him.

Ilse pointed towards the corkboard behind them. "See?"

"Yeah," Sawyer murmured. "They're blondes."

Ilse nodded quickly, pointing towards the single brown hair fiber smeared in the blood on the helmet. Not a particularly long strand of hair—perhaps from a male. The killer?

Sawyer was already clicking his fingers and gesturing for one of the lab techs to join them. "Bring an evidence bag," Sawyer said. He pointed at the hair follicle. "Need forensics to run a DNA test on that as fast as humanly possible."

The tech approached, wincing and shaking his head. "Normally that takes days," the man said.

"I don't care," Sawyer retorted. "Those kids might already be dead. We don't have days. Bag it, tag it, lab it. Got me?"

The man sighed but nodded slowly, unhooking a pair of tweezers from a small folding kit in one hand. As he knelt, Ilse and Sawyer regained their feet. Ilse felt her heart pounding rapidly. Was this the lucky break they'd been waiting for? What were the odds of a hair follicle being left behind?

She hesitated, frowning, staring towards the helmet.

It almost seemed too good to be true, and generally, in such cases, things *were* too good to be true.

She bit her lip, feeling a rising sense of uncertainty.

But Sawyer was still barking instructions. Now that kids were involved, he seemed to have hit a new gear. "I mean it," he was saying, "I want those results as fast as humanly possible. Twice as fast!"

***

Ilse was back in their car, sitting with one wheel on the curb where Sawyer had hopped it in his rush to reach the crime scene. State and local police were on a full-scale manhunt, along with a number of volunteers, evident by the flash of headlights and whirring sirens against the cloud cover of night.

Sawyer hadn't joined Ilse in the car, but instead was pacing the sidewalk, back and forth, raising his phone to check every few minutes if the DNA results had returned yet.

It was such a small thing to put so much hope on. A single hair follicle. They had no other leads. The searchers hadn't found anything yet either. What if the hair was from one of the twins' friends? What if Clyde or Penny had a pet they didn't know about.

Another officer was still interviewing the mother but thankfully had taken her back to the station. Ilse wasn't sure she could've continued sitting by while the woman had wept without comfort or compassion.

Still, Sawyer was right.

The best way to truly help her was to find her kids. Ilse drummed her fingers against the dashboard. She had other concerns cycling through her mind. The killer had been so careful up to this point. He hadn't left any evidence behind. If this hair was from him... had they just gotten lucky?

She knew it happened. No one could perfectly maintain every crime scene. In reality, murder was a messy business. Things went awry.

And yet still, Ilse had a sense of foreboding she couldn't quite quell.

Sawyer paced the sidewalk beneath a streetlight, but then suddenly froze, his eyes widening. He lifted his phone. Ilse's heart fluttered. But then Sawyer cursed, lowering the phone again and shaking his head in the direction of Ilse's parked car.

Not the lab.

And so the waiting continued. Sawyer did another circuit up and down the sidewalk outside the house. The whir of sirens were distancing further now.

Ilse closed her eyes for a moment, thinking through their next move. This was the only lead they had—if this didn't turn up anything, then the Denzel twins were as good as dead. Against the insides of her eyelids, she could see the images on the corkboard, just pressed there. Those young, beautiful lives couldn't end like this. She refused to let it.

She bit her tongue faintly, trying to use pain to focus.

In her mind's eye, she glimpsed a shadow lurking just beneath the corkboard. She glimpsed dark images drawing nearer in her thoughts. The twins were running out of time, and if they didn't hurry, there was nothing they could—

Tap! Tap!

Her eyes snapped open, her stomach lurching as she turned sharply. Sawyer was knocking on the window, his motions urgent, his phone pressed to his face. Ilse's own eyes widened, and she shoved open the door, narrowly avoiding clipping Tom on the leg.

He stepped back with the blow and kept speaking on the phone, watching Ilse as he did.

"You're sure? I know it was rushed, so are you at least *mostly* sure. Great... Yeah. Great." He paused, listening. Then Sawyer bobbed his head once. "Thanks. Send it."

He hung up.

Ilse met his gaze.

He looked back at his phone, waiting.

"Well?" she insisted.

He looked distractedly at the device in his hand before shooting her a sidelong glance. "Got a match. Hang on."

Ilse felt her heart skip. If Sawyer was calling it a *match,* that meant the strand of hair wasn't automatically ruled out. Which meant...

"Here," Sawyer said, stepping near and tilting his phone so she could see.

Ilse stared at the image on the device. The man in question was passably handsome, though his eyes ruined the illusion. Something about those eyes—too deeply set... too dark. Too cold. The face itself was nondescript. Dark hair, just like the strand they'd found. The man looked trim, athletic, his chin and jawbone more than pronounced.

"No record," Sawyer said, tapping a second of the document below the picture. "No priors. One arrest."

"An arrest?"

"Nearly fifteen years ago," Sawyer said with a nod.

"Hang on—what's this blank spot here?"

Sawyer tapped the phone, zooming in. He shook his head, running a hand over the back of his baseball cap. "Guy's a ghost," Tom muttered. "No online presence. No email."

Ilse fidgeted uncomfortably, tapping her fingers against the windowsill of the car. "So what's this arrest from fifteen years ago?"

"Umm...," Sawyer turned the phone now, skipping through the report's pages. Then, his eyebrows went up. "Huh. Interesting."

"What is?"

"They brought him in to question him for a murder."

"Wait, so was he arrested or just a suspect?"

"Looks like here they *wanted* to arrest, but there wasn't enough evidence."

As he said it, a cold shiver crept up Ilse's spine. She looked Sawyer dead in the eye. "Is that so?" she murmured.

He returned the look. "Guy is practically a nobody."

Ilse studied the name next to the picture. Guy Wolfe. "Hello, Mr. Wolfe," she murmured faintly, feeling her nerves still prickling across her skin. "So what case was he suspected in?"

"Murder of his mother, looks like. Mr. Wolfe's mom was brutally killed some time ago. He was questioned—only a teen at the time—but cops confirmed he and his abusive mother had been estranged for years."

"So Guy was released?"

"Right. Case left unsolved."

Ilse stared into the cold eyes of the figure on the screen. The man's mother was killed. The fellow himself had been a suspect in the brutal murder. Now three other victims attested to the brutality of their serial killer. Two teens had just been kidnapped. And the same man's hair was found at the crime scene.

She looked at the screen a second longer, staring into those deep-set, cold eyes. "I think we should head to his place," Ilse murmured softly, her voice shaking somewhat from the adrenaline now rushing through her system.

"Already got the address," Sawyer said, sliding over the hood and spinning into the passenger seat. "You drive. Let's go."

The door opened and slammed as Sawyer flung himself into the vehicle, and Ilse—without hesitation—turned the key, put the car in gear and pulled away from the curb. "Where to?" she said as the vehicle bounced off the sidewalk. "Call out directions if you think I'm going to miss. We're going fast, Tom."

CHAPTER TWENTY FOUR

"Of course," Ilse murmured as the GPS barked *arriving at destination on left.* She was now thirty miles outside Seattle. Ilse stared through the windshield at the small, wooden cabin set against a backdrop of mountainous forests. "Of course he lives in a cabin in the woods."

She felt her memories flitting back to her own experience in just such a home. The trees at night loomed around them, swelling across the dirt road. She felt exposed, all of a sudden. As if night itself were staring at her.

Ilse felt a flicker of anxiety, her hands so tight on the steering wheel one of her knuckles popped.

Sawyer just waited patiently as Ilse pulled to a halt outside the dusty cabin, and then he flung himself from the vehicle, marching up to the home. As he hastened forward, he suddenly went stiff. He frowned, glancing down at the ground.

Ilse moved as well, shaking badly, wishing to return to the car and hide. But hiding wasn't an option now. The twins were in danger. They might already be dead. Full steam ahead was the only option.

Still, as she moved through the shadowed trail beneath the dark branches, memories from little Hilda Mueller's own trek through a forest once upon a time came back to her. Ilse rubbed at her elbows, trying to fight off a slow chill.

Sawyer, though, was still standing stock still, holding out a hand over his shoulder.

"Wait," he barked suddenly, as she drew nearer.

She went still.

"What is it?"

Sawyer pointed at the ground. "Tripwire."

She blinked in surprise, but then leaned in and her eyes widened. A gossamer thin strand of wire stretched across the dirt driveway between two trees. Only the faintest hint of moonlight through tree cover dappling the road gave any indication something was there. She stared equal parts stunned at the tripwire itself, and also that Sawyer had even noticed it.

Sawyer followed the wire, moving along slowly towards one of the trees. Carefully, watching the detritus-strewn floor, Sawyer glanced behind the trunk.

"Huh," he said. "An alarm system," he murmured. He pointed up towards the branches. "Two cameras. See them?"

Ilse tried to make them out in the dark, but just shook her head. "Why," she murmured, "would an innocent man need a tripwire?"

Sawyer shrugged, rolling his shoulders. "Prepper in the woods?" he guessed. "Stay behind me, doc. Keep back."

The two of them stepped gingerly over the wire stretched between the trees. Ilse's apprehension was now at an all-time high. Her heart was pounding so loudly she thought it might collapse her chest. Her mind kept swimming with a million and one horrible possibilities of their plight. What if the killer was watching them now at the end of a sniper scope? What if the twins were in that cabin, cut to tiny pieces?

She gritted her teeth, trying to step behind Sawyer and keep up with his lanky strides. Even while moving cautiously, Sawyer had an excited energy about him.

He was not following the drive, preferring to step through the detritus and undergrowth of the forested area on either side. They reached the wooden steps of the cabin. The structure creaked from the faint wind and from old age. The beams of wood crisscrossing the threshold were tangled with cobwebs. Ilse spotted more than one fly trapped motionless in the webs.

Once Tom had made sure the steps weren't booby-trapped as well, he moved up them at a careful pace, gesturing, once he'd reached the top, for Ilse to join him.

Which she did, reluctantly, still full of anxiety that went down her spine and ended in a knot in her gut.

"Do we knock?" Ilse said in barely a whisper.

In answer, Sawyer just leaned in, peering through the windows framing the door. He hesitated, glancing through the darkened glass, then shrugged. He pushed a hand against the door, trying the handle gently at first. "No resistance," he murmured. He shrugged again and then twisted the handle and pushed.

The door creaked, opening slowly.

Ilse frowned, feeling a cavern open in her chest, a deep, dark emptiness. An ominous foreboding rising within. What sort of man placed a tripwire but left his door unlocked?

What sort of cautious killer left a hair fiber?

Something seemed off.

But she didn't have time to dwell on it as Sawyer was now stepping into the cabin, gesturing at her to follow.

They both emerged in a dark room with odd, wooden carved furniture visible from the faint moonlight. Sawyer clicked a flashlight on, sweeping it across the cold space. A long, epoxy-resin dining table made of wood and chemicals centered the space beneath a chandelier of jutting antlers woven together.

A large elk's head sat above a fireplace, staring with glassy eyes towards the newcomers.

Ilse shivered at the items. By the looks of things, Mr. Wolfe was a hunter. Hunters had guns. She heard the faintest snap as Sawyer unbuttoned his holster.

She glanced back at him, but he was already moving towards the two doors in the back of the space. The cabin was small, much smaller, even, than Ilse's apartment.

It didn't take Sawyer long to push open each door and clear the rooms. His flashlight shone like a lighthouse beacon, illuminating a single, empty bedroom, save a cot on the ground. And a bathroom with a sink but no shower.

The kitchen was behind one of the walls, hidden in shadow, out of sight from the main room with the large table and antler chandelier.

"Clear," Sawyer said after another sweep of his light *beneath* the table. He frowned, scratching at his chin. "Guy?" he called out, raising his voice now.

The two of them waited in the eerie dark, listening to the creak of wood. But there was no response. No sound except for the interruptions of wind and wood.

"Not here," Sawyer said, looking back at Ilse. He studied her with his green eyes as if waiting for her to reach some conclusion.

Ilse bit her lip, thinking desperately. Mr. Wolfe was their killer—she felt certain of it. Certainty was more an emotional sense at times, but other times it came with a bone-deep *knowing.* This man was their killer. But also... also...

Why did it almost feel like he was toying with them? As if they were wandering into some game without even realizing it. Why had he left a hair fiber behind? Why was it so easy to find his cabin? Why had the door been unlocked?

And now, where was Mr. Wolfe? More importantly, where were the Denzel twins?

“Shit, Ilse,” Sawyer said sharply, causing prickles to erupt across her arms.

“What?” she demanded, slipping back into the skin she'd nearly jumped out of.

“Look! Look here!” Sawyer was tapping a finger at the table, his eyes the size of quarters.

Prompted by the urgency in his tone, Ilse hastened forward, peering down at the indicated portion of the wood surface. She blinked, studying it, feeling her blood bruit as if at a quickened pace. Someone had carved words into the table with a knife.

Recently too, judging by the peeled strands of wood.

The words were in phrases, listed. The first was clear: *Gingerbread Man. Arthur.*

Ugly Duckling. Adelaide.

Jack and the Beanstalk. Lee Jackson.

Hansel and Gretel.

The final title didn't have a name next to it. But the other three names had all been crossed out as if with a red marker. Ilse stared at the words and names etched in the wood. She felt a rising sense of terror followed by the stunned realization that this confirmed it.

“See,” she murmured. “It is him.”

Sawyer just stared at the names, scowling. He looked at her, didn't apologize, but did give a faint nod. “Yup,” he said. Then he went quiet, watching her, waiting. After a moment, trying to gather her thoughts, Ilse realized this was Sawyer's version of deference. He was holding his tongue now. Not quite an apology, but at least a willingness to let her take the lead. She'd been right.

But what did it matter if she couldn't find the missing kids?

Why had the killer just etched the names on his dining room table? It all seemed so... contrived. Intentional.

Like a trail of breadcrumbs.

Ilse pressed her tongue against her lower lip if only for the sense of something sturdy. She glanced faintly around, studying the table, the rest of the room, searching for... for another breadcrumb?

Then she spotted something. More gouge marks on the table, but this time in the epoxy rather than the wood. She frowned, leaning in, and her eyes suddenly widened.

“Tom...” she said slowly. “Look!”

He did, leaning in also. The two of them both stared, desperately trying to make sense of the markings just beneath the resin surface of the table.

There, in the blue and green swirls of the resin, *beneath* the smooth varnished surface, Ilse spotted more marks. More X's across the wood.

And also, nearly invisible, next to the X's, she spotted the names of locations. *Caspen Studios.* An X next to it. Then, a foot off the right, she read *Central Park,* and another X. Then, her eyes traveled to the very edge of the table. Another mark beneath the surface, and this one read, *Jackson's farm.* And another X.

"Shit," Sawyer said suddenly. "Ilse—Ilse I think it's a damn map. He's left us a map. That's where he killed them. Those three marks. It's a confession. He did it. Holy—"

"There's a fourth," Ilse said suddenly, pointing. Another X mark, this time off to the left of to the Northeast of the rest of the marks. Ilse hesitated, frowning, trying to piece together the geography in her brain. This mark was in green resin...

"That's this forest," she said suddenly, tapping her finger. "He's here. Somewhere. In the woods, in the mountains. Tom, shit, he's nearby!" She spun around, facing Sawyer, her eyes blazing. "He's going to kill them in this forest!"

"Damn it."

"How big is the wood here?" Ilse asked, desperately.

"Hundreds of square miles, Ilse."

She winced, but then pointed towards the X mark. "Where is that?" she said.

Sawyer shrugged. "Even if the map is to scale, it could cover any amount of space. A thousand acres, maybe more."

Ilse gritted her teeth, glancing once more to the empty bathroom, then the bedroom as if convincing her subconscious he wasn't just standing in the empty rooms. She huffed and then said, "We need to contact the search parties. Reroute them. Get them all in the woods—everyone. Two together. Make sure they're armed." She glanced towards the elk head over the wall and shivered. "He damn well is going to be."

Sawyer was already pulling his phone, placing the call to dispatch to reorient the searchers.

Ilse walked quickly, with stiff steps, but then broke into a jog. "Come on!" she called. "I need your flashlight.

"--Right now," she heard Sawyer saying hurriedly. "I'm sending coordinates. All of them! Yes, dammit, everyone. No time—just send them!"

Then as she rushed out the door, taking the steps hurriedly, she heard the sound of Sawyer giving rapid pursuit.

She faced the trees, closing her eyes for a moment and picturing the table with the X mark. If it was to scale then... then the killer would be...

"That direction!" Sawyer was saying, rushing past her, his flashlight waving back and forth. He jammed a finger towards a dirt road leading away from the house. "Come on, doc! This way—the rest are coming."

Ilse's lips felt suddenly dry. For a moment, she felt as if she'd discovered a tripwire of her own. Here, amidst the driveway, near a cabin, she was *near* the forest without quite being *in* it. But the trail, leading away, through the woods?

It was like something out of a storybook. She'd endured such a story before. She'd wandered away from a trail in the past. People had died then. Two people, in fact—her brothers. Little Hilda Mueller had gotten lost in the woods, and people had died.

She stared, eyes wide in their sockets at the trees around her. Her heart hammered so wildly she wanted to scream.

"Doc!" Sawyer shouted back, waving the flashlight in her direction. "I think I see ATV tracks! You coming?"

Now wasn't the time for hesitation. It wasn't the time for fear. Sometimes, all that remained wasn't the certainty of an outcome, but the courage leading up to a conclusion.

Courage wasn't the absence of fear. At least, that's what some said.

If this was the case, then Ilse was filled with every opportunity to be courageous imaginable. All she felt was terror. Not just the fear of the moment, or what lay beyond. Not even the fear of confronting a brutal torturer in the woods.

But other fears. Dormant fears.

Would she react under pressure? Or would she freeze up?

Too many questions... Too many thoughts. She gritted her teeth, muttering beneath her breath, "Three victims. Guy Wolfe. Brown hair. Dead eyes."

Then, she picked up the pace, stepping over her own imaginary tripwire and rushing after Sawyer and his bobbing flashlight into the woods.

CHAPTER TWENTY FIVE

Night fell, and the trees grew larger, and Ilse's heart seemed to shrink in her chest. Occasionally, she heard the squawk of Sawyer's radio in his belt as the arriving search parties notified them of their locations. Sawyer, though, only answered enough to give curt instructions to the new arrivals. Hundreds of square miles, only twenty or so searchers.

They had their work cut out for them.

Ilse was on the verge of a nervous breakdown. She hated to admit it, but she wasn't nearly as over her own trauma as she wanted to think. Trauma didn't control her, didn't dominate her life. She refused to let it. But when it *did* show up, it whispered lies in her ears. *I'm all you are. You'll never be free.*

This, she knew rationally, wasn't true. The trauma grew less, her strength more, the PTSD fading. Her life was wonderful, if she took a moment to think about it. Not just professionally, but also personally. She had dear friends like Dr. Mitchell, and even Sawyer. She enjoyed her work. Loved her clients.

But sometimes, every now and then, it would all be threatened by memories of a past she'd long left behind.

It wasn't a successful professional in her thirties following Sawyer through the dark now, but a seven-year-old German girl with an unusual name.

Her eyes were wide, and Ilse kept glancing side to side.

Sawyer was following what he called *tracks* in the dust. To Ilse, it was little more than the occasional bump in the dirt. But Sawyer seemed certain and continued to pick up the pace, hurrying faster and faster.

Suddenly, a voice squawked over Sawyer's belt-radio. *"We're at the cabin. Agent Sawyer. Hello, come in Agent Sawyer."*

Tom scowled, paused, clicked the radio and barked. "Follow the trail," he snapped. His tone suggested the word *duh.*

Though Ilse could never imagine the man actually *saying* the word. Still, he clicked the radio receiver down, turning the volume as low as possible while still allowing the searchers to contact him. He paused, glancing back over his shoulder down the path they'd taken through the deep woods.

"You okay?" he said at last, looking towards Ilse.

She winced, flashing a thumbs up, but didn't reply right away—it took all her energy just to remember to breathe properly.

He looked at her, his hard expression softening for a moment, caught by the glow of the flashlight in his hand. "Here," he said, "You hold this." He handed the light to her.

Ilse hesitated, but then took it, feeling a surge of gratitude. She shone the light through the trees around her, illuminating the thick underbrush and the even thicker trunks, ridged with bark. Wherever she shone the light, illuminating the forest, things seemed less eerie somehow. Less frightening. Just branches and twigs and leaves and moss...

She found she was breathing a bit easier.

"Thanks," she muttered.

Sawyer pretended like he hadn't heard. Pretended, she guessed, like he hadn't noticed the sweat on her forehead, or the unblinking widening of her eyes, or the panting of her breath.

He just gave her a look, patted her on the shoulder, said, "I'm right here. We got this, yeah? Shine the light this way. I think I see something."

Ilse felt another flash of gratitude and swallowed a lump in her throat. She pointed the light in the direction Tom had indicated, and he clicked his tongue, leaping forward suddenly and pointing. "Aha!" he said. "Look."

She did, and then she frowned. A piece of fabric was lopped over a branch, torn and frayed. Sawyer's eyebrows rose. "We're on the right track," he said, slowly placing the fabric back on the branch. He scuffed the dirt beneath the branch with his foot. "Would draw a sign if I could," he muttered. "Others will walk right past it otherwise." He shook his head in irritation at the lack of observational skills he found in others.

Ilse, though, was frowning for different reasons. Another breadcrumb. It seemed too... easy?

An unlocked door. A hair fiber. A fragment of clothing.

She closed her eyes for a moment, keeping the flashlight raised so she could feel the glow of the light against her skin, inside her eyelids. In the fairy tale, Hansel and Gretel were lost in the woods and came across a witch's house. Breadcrumbs were left to help find the kids... A trail.

If the killer really was reenacting the fairy tales, then there had to be a building or a structure nearby. Perhaps not quite a witch's house, but at least some place to reenact the tale.

Ilse glanced at the sky, frowning towards the moon through the trees. They were running out of time. The twins had already been missing for hours. The killer could easily have disposed of them already. She glanced at Tom. "Do you get GPS out here?"

"Hmm? Yeah, why?"

"Can you look for any buildings nearby? Structures of any kind. Just somewhere he might have taken them."

"What if he's just in the woods somewhere? Some hidey-hole, like that creepy skin-stuffer we caught."

Ilse winced. "I—I think he'll try and stay as close to the story as possible. At least... I hope so." She shrugged.

"What about this?" Sawyer said, pointing to the fabric.

Ilse paused, staring at it, then looked back at Sawyer. She didn't speak for a moment, trying to process through her own threat of panic, but Sawyer seemed to be able to study her expression. He frowned now, his green-eyes flashing in the light. "Hmm, yeah. Bit too easy, right? That's what I was thinking too. Think he's leading us on a wild goose chase?"

"I don't know," Ilse said, still somewhat panting. "But if we find nearby structures, somewhere in the woods, we might be able to find the twins before it's too late."

Sawyer huffed, but then said, "My phone won't be good enough. Here, hang on—let's see if the peanut gallery can do something useful for a change."

Sawyer reached for his radio, turning the volume back up, then rocking on his heels. He gritted his teeth, listening to chatter on the line for a moment. Comments like, *"Taking north third. Dawkins, you take west fourth. Quadrant patterns, guys. Stick to it!"*

Sawyer waited for this to end, before raising his voice and saying, "Hello, dispatch? You copy? Anyone with a SAT phone or onboard GPS—I need some eyes!"

"Who is this?" a voice replied.

"This is Agent Sawyer," Tom snapped. "You got what I need?"

This voice went quiet, and Sawyer rolled his eyes, standing with one hand on his hip beneath the trees, illuminated solely by the flashlight in Ilse's hand. Thankfully, a second later, a new, fainter voice said, “What do you need, Tom?”

Sawyer blinked. “Rawley?”

“Yes, Agent Sawyer. How can I help?”

Ilse blinked, impressed. She had to hand it to the supervising agent. Despite Sawyer's intense dislike of the man, for whatever reason, Agent Rawley seemed willing to do even the tough jobs that most supervisors might prefer to assign their subordinates.

Sawyer winced for a second, but then stowing personal pride, he said, “Structures. Anything near us. I'll send you my coordinates. Give me outbuildings, cabins, radio towers—whatever.”

“Parameters?” Rawley returned.

“Fifty-mile radius to start,” Sawyer returned.

Ilse fidgeted uncomfortably. If they really were following the killer's tracks, he couldn't be *too* far ahead, surely. Unless he was just playing with them.

The two of them waited beneath the creak of the branches as the radio went silent. Most of the chatter had faded as well now as people made space for supervising Agent Rawley's response. A few moments passed before, at last, the radio crackled again.

“Agent Sawyer?” Rawley said. “Can you hear me?”

“Yeah. Got anything?”

“Three structures. One of them is twenty miles from your location. I'm sending Sharp's search party that way.”

“The other two?” Sawyer said.

“Near enough. Four miles and seven.”

Sawyer hesitated, and Ilse felt a faint chill along her spine.

“Four and seven?” Sawyer asked. “Near each other?”

“I'm afraid not—they're in opposite directions. I can send you coordinates. But Tom, I'm advising you wait for the other search parties to—”

“Send them,” Sawyer interrupted. “And be quick. We don't have time to wait.”

Sawyer lowered the radio volume again, and Rawley's response faded to little more than a soft purr lost in the breeze. Sawyer looked Ilse dead in the eyes. “What should we do?” he said.

Ilse bit her lip and glanced over her shoulder. The search teams had shown up late. They were already running behind. Some as much as half an hour. Sawyer and Ilse had been navigating in the dark for a good amount of time already. If they tried to wait, they would only be wasting precious time.

Two structures in the woods. That's what Rawley had said.

Two possible locations.

Ilse fidgeted uncomfortably. Sawyer's phone buzzed, and he glanced down, studying the text for a moment. Then he glanced back up the path as if gauging something for himself. He sighed, then said, "One of the structures is a few miles down this path," he said. "An old shed near a water tower."

"The other?" Ilse asked.

He gestured off in the opposite direction, through the trees, away from the path. "That way. A bit further."

Ilse knew what they had to do but hated admitting it. Sawyer, to his credit, was waiting, allowing her to reach her own conclusion. The two of them had a head-start on everyone else. The twins were in jeopardy. The killer was out here, somewhere, biding his time. Perhaps even watching them at that moment.

A prickle crept up Ilse's spine, and she turned slowly, looking to the trees and frowning. But only swaying shadows in the gloom met her speculation.

"We...," she caught the words, her throat tight. She swallowed, trying again, "We should split—split up," she finished with a stammer.

Even as she said it, she loathed herself for it. But what else could she say? She knew it was true. They had to split up—they had to go separate directions. If they wanted a chance of catching the killer before he finished the twins, they couldn't dawdle. Certainly not out of simple fear. Ilse's own mental state couldn't be the reason these kids died. She'd never forgive herself.

So she summoned what residue of courage remained, and said, more fervently, "We need to split up."

Sawyer just studied her. "You sure?"

"Yeah. Yes—yes..."

"Right," Tom said. He glanced at her with something akin to admiration in his gaze. "You head down this path. Don't get off it. The water tower and shed will be visible in a couple of miles. Go slow, don't hurt yourself. Call immediately if you see anything. Got it?"

Ilse bit her lip but nodded once. "And you?"

"I'll do the same, this way. I'm quicker moving through the woods anyway. Hopefully the slowpokes will catch up soon enough."

He winced and shrugged.

"Maybe... Maybe he'll be at that third structure Rawley mentioned?" Ilse said hopefully. "The one he's sending—"

“Sharp's search team? Yeah. Maybe. Good luck, doc. Remember, stay quiet, stay low, call immediately if you need anything. Got it?” Sawyer began to turn, but then paused, looking back at Ilse. “Doc,” he said slowly. “This guy has already tortured three people to death. Don't be slow on the draw...,” he looked her in the eyes. “Catch my meaning?”

Ilse hesitated, feeling her fingers prickle on the tips. She didn't want to think about shooting someone. Didn't want, at all, to think about a solitary sojourn through the woods. But now wasn't the time for comfort. Now it was action's turn.

She nodded once, and this time Sawyer just waited and watched, letting her turn and begin to move first. She flashed the light along the path, picking slowly along the trail at first, but then hastening forward with each step. The light swayed and swished in front of her, scanning the ground.

Just stick to the trail. That's what he said. How hard could it be?

The same trail where they'd found a discarded piece of clothing. Was she being led into a trap?

She winced, hesitant and glanced back. But Sawyer was gone now, too. She spotted a second, smaller light, probably from his phone, shining through the trees as Tom moved in the opposite direction.

Part of her wanted to call out for him. To get him to come back and help her. But another part of her knew this was the right call. Time was ticking. Splitting up could cover more distance. She'd trained for this, hadn't she?

She only felt like a child. Really, she was a woman who'd faced far worse than a nighttime stroll through the woods.

She swallowed faintly, but looked back to the trail, light on the ground. She stalked forward, head down, heart hammering, doing her best to say on the path.

CHAPTER TWENTY SIX

One foot in front of the other, leaving curls of dust on the air behind her, Ilse made her way down the trail, through the dark. As she continued along, Ilse spotted no additional signs. No fabric, no bent branches, nothing she might have imagined as a sort of breadcrumb trail leading her through the night.

Perhaps she was on the wrong path, after all?

Ilse was ashamed to realize this thought filled her with a sense of huge relief. She didn't want to encounter the killer, didn't want to come across him in the dark woods while on her own.

But still, despite her fear, she took another step. Another.

And that's when she spotted it. Up ahead.

She paused at the end of a switchback, peering through low branches in the direction of the shed. The water tower itself was little more than a rusted duck blind with a tank on top. The legs of the tower were rusted straight through, and one was missing entirely as if the metal post had been carted away.

But Ilse's eyes fixated on the shed. Exactly where Sawyer had said it would be.

***

Sawyer sprinted through the woods like a bat out of hell. He'd been forced to navigate the vehicle-inaccessible terrain in the dark with little more than faint illumination and instinct to guide him. Small branches tugged at his sleeves as he hastened forward. Ahead, he spotted the abandoned, old oil-rig monitoring outbuilding.

The windows were smashed. Dust carpeted the floor. He didn't slow as he jogged up old, moldered wooden steps and reached the door.

This was also broken—missing entirely in fact. The hinges were gone too. Metal scavengers.

The place smelled of urine and rot and looked as if no one had visited it in a decade.

"This isn't it," he muttered to himself, breathing heavily as he stared into the small outbuilding. This wasn't the building. The dust didn't lie.

No footprints, no disturbance, just a thin layer of dust. His heart pounded, and he stepped into the single room building, staring at the unfurnished space. Scavengers had been by months if not years before. Everything had been picked clean, including wiring in the walls judging by holes where outlets might have gone.

This wasn't the lair. This wasn't where the murderer had gone.

"Damn it," he growled beneath his breath. But he said nothing further, as he was already on his heel, picking up the pace. He took the steps in one long stride and hit the dusty ground running. Ilse was heading into an unknown location. If this wasn't the killer's lair, and the third party hadn't heard anything, then that meant Ilse was in danger.

He broke into a sprint, racing rapidly through the trees once more in the opposite direction.

***

But now, the orange glow through the windows of the small structure caused prickles to tremble across Ilse's spine. Her eyes bulged as she stared at the small shed. It looked like a cross between a garage and an enormous outhouse with windows. Perhaps used for ranger's tools, or maintenance on the tower.

Whatever the case, the shed itself also looked long abandoned. Moldered, blackened wood seemed equal parts mush and neglect. The thing didn't look as if it should have been standing.

Ilse frowned at the glow of light, though, coming from within.

Had she found him?

Her lips were numb and with trembling fingers she fished her phone from her pocket, raising it and hastily dialing Sawyer's number.

She waited in the dark, beneath the sheltering branches of a tree, her heart somewhere in the vicinity of her toes and neck all at once.

She waited as the phone tried to connect.

But all she received was a dial tone.

Ilse bit her lip, and growled beneath her breath, trying to call Sawyer a second time. But again, quicker this time, she was met by a busy tone.

She stared at her screen, the looked at the small bars in the top left. Only one remained, red. Critical. She had lost reception.

Ilse felt an emotion normally accompanying nightmares now, descending on her like a damp, woolen blanket. She raised her phone, jutting it skyward in an attempt to find reception. But no luck. Even the final, red bar vanished on her dumb, flip phone. Sawyer had the radio, which was connected to his own phone so he could coordinate the search.

"Shit!" she hissed beneath her breath. "God dammit." She stood breathing heavily, chest rising and falling. She wanted to leave.

Now, more than ever, she wanted to turn and run.

She was well and truly alone.

Suddenly, it struck her how stupid it had been to split with Sawyer. She never should have suggested it.

On the other hand... what if the twins were already dead? What if... but what if... what if they were still clinging on? What if there was still time?

She'd come this way for them, hadn't she? Not for herself, but for them.

She stared towards the small, illuminated shed beneath the old, three-legged rusted water tanker. She wanted to scream and run. But again, summoning her resolve, with shaky steps, she moved forward again, pressing through the threat of night, through the foreboding sense threatening to drown her.

She gripped her dead phone in one hand and then jammed the offending device deep into her pocket. No use for that thing now. Technology was evil anyway.

Just then, as she moved slowly towards the illuminated shed, she spotted a flicker. Ilse frowned, staring at the windows. The light continued to flicker, and Ilse suddenly realized the illumination was from some sort of fire... or perhaps a candle or lantern.

But the flickering light also cast odd shadows against the window, from the inside. Ilse just stared at these, adrenaline now rushing through her body.

The curtains were closed, but thanks to the flicker of light, she now spotted them: silhouettes. Vague outlines of figures *inside the shed.*

And then, if that wasn't enough to prompt her forward, a faint mewling voice echoed from the cabin. "H—help!" the voice called, straining.

The silhouettes didn't move as if frozen stiff, or, perhaps, rigid in fear.

"P-please, help!" the same voice called, echoing in the dark.

Ilse couldn't wait any longer. No reception, isolated in a dark forest, with search teams twenty or more minutes behind her. She didn't have twenty minutes. Judging by the desperation in the voice ahead, neither did the woman in the cabin.

Ilse's gaze fixated on the two silhouettes, and she moved forward, slower than she might have liked, as if plodding through mud, one ungainly step at a time. The fear pressed around her; the trees witnessed the spectacle of someone shuddering more than the leaves on their branches.

And yet Ilse's hand moved to the weapon at her hip. She pulled it carefully, her shaking fingers pressed to the rigid and unyielding metal. She knew she could do this. She *had* to do this.

"Come on," she muttered to herself. "Come on!"

She suddenly broke into a jog. She wasn't sure where this surge of energy came from—she'd thought she'd already spent all of her adrenaline.

Now, though, she rushed forward. Tripwires? She didn't care—didn't see any. But mostly she knew if she stopped to look, she wouldn't do anything, she'd remain rooted in place.

The last time she'd delayed in a forest, her two brothers had been killed. Punishment by her father and her stepmother for their help in getting little Hilda to escape. She'd been told to fetch help, told to bring police. But three weeks she'd delayed.

Hilda had gotten lost in the woods. Ilse still couldn't remember those days—those horrible, horrible moments wandering barefoot through the dark.

She rushed forward now, towards the shed with the flickering candlelight. Towards the silhouettes still motionless and terrifyingly rigid. The sound of the voice was fading now. A young voice. She was sure of it.

"Penny!" Ilse cried. An instant later, she wished she'd kept her silence. But no doubt the killer was already alerted to her presence. She needed to rescue the twins! Needed to save her sibling—no... no not her siblings.

She slammed into the shed door, shoulder first. For a painful moment, she thought she might just ricochet off, but then the door buckled, bent and swung in with a clatter.

Ilse stood in the doorway, eyes wide, gun in hand, panting so heavily it sounded like the swishing ocean in her ears.

Except now that she faced the small shed, staring within, she realized her mistake.

A poker table with chips on top. And the two figures she'd spotted sitting at it... mannequins. Lifeless, plastic faces stared at each other over the green felt of the table. A candle had been set up behind the two mannequins, casting their shadows against the curtains.

Ilse stared for a moment at the scene, swallowing.

Then, a voice echoed out. “Help me... Please...”

It took her a second to locate the source of the sound. Gun still gripped in one hand, her eyes darted to the small radio sitting on the table. She stared, gulping air. The radio went suddenly silent.

There she stood, alone with two mannequins for company, a flickering candle and a radio used for no other reason than as a decoy.

She'd been had.

Ilse felt a prickle along the nape of her neck. She turned sharply, glancing back towards the forest. No motion. No movement.

Then, she heard a creak of wood. Ilse's lips tightened. “Who's there?” she demanded, whirling around again, sweeping the shed with her sights. But she spotted no one. “I said who's there?” she yelled at the top of her lungs.

Ilse kept her gun in quavering fingers and heard another creak of wood. This time coming from the opposite direction. She whirled on a darker portion of the shed. But still spotted no movement. No figure. Just darkness.

A ghost?

What a silly thought. Like something out of a storybook.

“Hello, friend,” said a voice suddenly, bursting from the radio on the table.

She stared at it, breathing wildly.

“Yes, yes,” the voice said over the radio, “I can see you. You're a dark-haired lady in a sweater. See? I can see. I can hear you too. You breathe loudly, don't you?”

Ilse didn't reply, shifting her step so her back was to the wall now. She turned faintly towards the ceiling, checking for cameras. Her terror had reached a climax. She wanted to melt into the wall, to disappear. She'd thought the shed might provide some solace from the encroaching forest, but now she'd found another type of horror. Her memories, her recollections surfaced through the turgid water of her mind. She couldn't escape. Couldn't hold it back.

So, she allowed some of the fear to tinge her voice with rage.

“Guy Wolfe, is that you?” she demanded.

The radio crackled and the voice just chuckled. She heard another creak. And this time, she tilted her head sharply, staring straight up.

Someone was on the roof.

Someone had been hiding on the roof, and now they were moving. She tucked her tongue inside her cheek, biting down so she wouldn't scream. She tasted coppery blood. Tasted salt.

But he could see her, and she couldn't see him.

She heard another creak of a footstep. He was directly above her now. She knew that much. Slowly, she began to raise her gun.

"I'm not impressed," the voice on the radio said, congenially. "Not at all. I left that hair. I wanted you to find me. What's your name?"

Ilse felt a flicker of vindication. So she'd been right. He'd been leaving clues.

"Breadcrumbs?" she murmured. "Like in the stories?"

The voice suddenly sounded excited, the tone changing all at once. "You like the stories too?" he said.

Ilse just waited, listening.

"I love them," he said merrily. "They're some of my favorite... Well, sometimes. Happy endings though—they're somewhat cheap, aren't they?"

Something had changed now that Ilse had mentioned a specific of the fairy tales. She raised her gun, pointing it at the roof. The voice over the receiver said, "Stop that. If you shoot me, they die."

She hesitated, finger on the trigger, eyes wide, simply staring at the inside of a dusty, wooden shed roof.

The voice didn't sound scared at all. As if it couldn't experience fear.

"Why are you doing this?" Ilse murmured.

"Doing? I'm not doing anything. I'm just part of the story," the voice said cheerfully. "Here, hang on a moment, don't shoot. Let's talk."

She heard a sudden thump, and whirled around, eyes open in horror to find a handsome man had dropped from the roof and was now standing on the wooden rail, one hand balanced against a load-bearing beam. He smirked at her, dropped into a sitting position on the rail then wiggled his fingers in a sort of playful wave.

The man matched his photo. Sharp cheekbones, a strong jaw but cold, dead eyes like a snake. He stared at her with that strange smirk as if he had all the time in the world. He didn't even seem to notice her gun. Or if he had noticed it, he didn't care.

She, on the other hand, was grateful for the weapon. She raised it, pointing at his head. "Don't move," she snapped. "Mr. Wolfe, you're under arrest."

He nodded along with her congenially. "Makes sense, makes sense," he said. "I haven't seen you before. Are you one of the good guys?" He wagged his feet where he sat, causing them to swish back and forth beneath the wooden rail.

Ilse scowled. "Yes," she said simply. "Which makes you a bad guy. Where are the twins?"

"Hmm? Oh, Hansel and Gretel?"

"Where are they, Guy! Did you hurt them already?"

He crossed his arms now, and Ilse noticed he was wearing black gloves. "Not yet," he said simply. "I can't decide if they deserve a happy ending or not, you know. It's a big decision." He wagged his head energetically. "Maybe you can help."

Ilse licked her chapped lips slowly, taking a step forward, gun still in hand. She was just within the shed's door, only a few paces away from where he sat on the wooden rail. "Get on the ground, *now,*" she said, channeling her inner Sawyer. "I mean it, or I'll shoot."

He looked her in the eyes. "Will you? Hmm... Maybe." But he remained exactly where he'd been sitting. "I suppose it's not too important to me one way or the other," he murmured. "You see, it's an important thing to have happily ever after, isn't it? So many people get their happy, but they cheat. It's not fair to cheat."

Ilse just stared at him. "That girl cut her face," he said conversationally. "That man used steroids."

"The model? The marathon runner?"

"And I don't have to mention the farmer, do I?" he said. He tutted and shook his head. "Not a nice person."

"And what did Penny and Clyde ever do?" she demanded. She could study the pores in the man's cheek through the sights on her gun. Her finger itched on the trigger.

"Oh, who?"

"Hansel and Gretel?" she asked through gritted teeth.

"Oh, them? Nothing yet."

"So that's it, hmm?" Ilse asked, scowling. "You kill them out of some twisted sense of justice?"

He raised an eyebrow at her, looking amused. "Someone has to, obviously. Do you know something—I've never told anyone this, but I think I can trust you... I did the same for my mother. Years ago."

"You were a suspect then too," Ilse snapped. "They just didn't have enough evidence."

"No, I suppose they wouldn't have. She was not a nice woman. Not at all."

"Where are the twins?"

"I'll get to that." His expression flickered into a frown.

Ilse wasn't sure what to do. He wasn't aggressing, wasn't running, but he also wasn't complying. She kept her gun trained on him, taking another step forward, just inside the threshold of the door.

"Coming closer, I see," he muttered. "Let me guess, you're falling for me, hmm? I really am quite good-looking." He winked, "Think of me as prince charming."

Ilse couldn't get a read on the man. He was clearly a narcissist. But he also didn't exhibit fear or anxiety. Either he had the best poker face imaginable, second only to the mannequins behind her, or something was off with him. Something twisted.

He'd murdered his mother, and while he hadn't gone into details, Ilse knew enough cases of her own to know how much a parent's abuse, and the subsequent trauma, could put someone on the wrong path unless they chose to fight it. Sometimes, the fight just didn't seem worthwhile. A fight like that seemed... unfair, almost. Why should someone experience pain for another person's choices?

And yet before her was the example of someone who had continued down the traumatic path. And now... now three people were dead. If not five.

Shit. She thought to herself. He was clearly stalling.

"I said," she put iron behind those words. "Get on the ground!"

He wagged his finger at her. "You know, you're starting to annoy me." His nose wrinkled. "In fact, you sound just like *her.* Get in that attic, Guy! Don't come until I tell you to, boy!" He screamed these words, his voice twisting now, going gruff.

He gave a shake of his head in disgust. "What was I supposed to do?" he demanded. "She was bigger. Older. My mother. So of course, I went into that attic. Locked away. Reading those stories again and again and again and again...," he rolled his finger as if to say etc.

Ilse blinked, still unsure how to react. He simply wasn't obeying. Should she shoot him? She remembered Sawyer's admonishment. The man had already killed three. The twins were still in danger. But... but he wasn't threatening her. He wasn't really doing anything except talking. It didn't seem right to shoot him. But perhaps that was why she'd started out as a counselor rather than an agent. She didn't have the same killer instinct as Sawyer.

But if she didn't pull the trigger, and he really was just stalling, then she was wasting precious time in subduing the threat.

She took another careful, hesitant step forward, the floor creaking beneath her.

"Of course, she apologized," the man prattled on, still kicking his feet like a child on a swing set. "Years later. Told me she'd changed. She'd gotten married. Started a new life." The man's eyes narrowed, and he shook his head. "The witch was *happy,*" he spat, the scorn all too evident in his voice. "Happy because she'd moved on... But I couldn't. I'd spent years under her rule. She was the wicked witch, you know! And so I couldn't just sit by and let her... let her enjoy her cruel reign. I knew I had to put a stop to it. So I did! See? I had to, so I did!"

Ilse felt a flicker of fear at the man's words. Part of her wanted to ignore his ravings completely. Another part, though, resonated with it. What would Ilse do if her stepmother came, or even her father, and apologized to her, said they had turned over a new leaf and wanted to move on, happily ever after?

She certainly wouldn't be able to live with it. Where would the justice be? After everything her father had done to them, to all of them, along with his mistress, Ilse wasn't sure there was ever forgiveness for it. She sometimes felt all too willing to forgive and rehabilitate those who had harmed another, but those who'd harmed her? Her sisters? Her brothers?

That was a different question entirely, and the apparent hypocrisy caused her stomach to turn. Ilse took another step forward, gun still raised.

And that's when she saw him smile.

He winked at her, waving his gloved fingers again. And then he flung himself backwards, rolling off the rail and out of the line of fire. At the same time, she saw his hand yank something beneath the rail. A dangling chain, like the sort attached to an old-fashioned toilet's water tank. The floor creaked beneath her. Then a wooden panel fell out completely.

You're falling for me.

That's what he'd said. The bastard.

Ilse shouted, trying to grab the edge of the floor as she plummeted through the ground. Her head struck the wood. Her gun went skittering. Splinters gouged into her fingers as she fell, kicking and struggling and desperately trying to shout.

But the sound was lost as she turned once, shoulder and headfirst, striking the ground with a painful *smack.*

She blinked, feeling blood welling down her forehead. Her shoulder had absorbed most of the fall, thankfully. She was still thinking, which meant there was something remaining to think with, mercifully.

As she lay there, trying to draw breath, to blink, she realized darkness was closing in. She heard murmured whispers, tearful voices above her. She heard a sound. Then someone said in a faint tone.

"Lady? Hey, lady, you okay?"

But that was it. The darkness pressed in; her heart throbbed. The bastard had dropped her through a trap door. He'd been goading her all along. He was still playing his game, and she'd fallen for it. Literally.

The voice faded suddenly into a whimper of terror. Ilse blinked and light suddenly flared against her eyelids. For a moment, the sudden interruption of the dark goaded her back to consciousness. She lay there, bleeding, blinking, desperate. And then, a shadow fell over her again. She heard footsteps, a soft murmur.

And the voice of Guy Wolfe whispered, "Nice of you to drop in, stranger."

CHAPTER TWENTY SEVEN

Ilse blinked, the pain in her head immense. But the splitting headache was the least of her concerns. As her consciousness returned, she felt the bindings around her wrists chaffing against her skin. Her arms were pulled behind her back.

She felt the sticky stain of blood along her temple, down her forehead, holding her hair against her skin. She groaned, her eyes blinking, and she looked desperately around the room.

As she came to, and her vision returned, she bit her tongue again, tasting stale blood. The pain in her head and mouth faded to horror.

Two figures were tied onto chairs against the wall. All three of them were in a basement, or a cellar, by the looks of things, beneath the shed. Dusty tools and old pickling jars rested on cobweb covered shelves. A low, flickering glow filled the pace. A couple of old bags of flour sat on the lower shelves. One of the bags had ripped, leaving a dusty powder across portions of the ground.

Ilse twisted, to try and take in more of her surroundings, but as she did, she felt something tap her cheek. One of the twins, the curly-haired girl, let out a faint whimper. Her eyes bugged as she stared over Ilse's shoulder towards someone behind her.

The faint tap on her cheek moved to her ear, and Ilse felt her hair pushed back. "Now, now," a voice whispered, "what did this to such a pretty ear? You didn't do it to yourself, did you?"

Ilse felt shivers of terror along her spine. The killer was standing out of sight, behind her, but so close she could feel the warm prickle of his breath against the nape of her neck, like the whisper of a lover.

But all she felt now was revulsion and terror.

She tested her mouth, the tangy taste of salt and copper swallowed down a dry throat. "You're making a mistake," she said, her voice rasping.

"Hmm? No, no, that's *you,* lady. I've been a step ahead of you this entire time." The killer stayed out of sight, still tracing something sharp against the side of her face. Judging by the look of horror in Penny's eyes, it wasn't anything nice. Clyde refused to look, staring at his legs. The boy's jeans were scuffed and torn as if he'd been dragged through dirt. He also had blood caking the side of his face. Penny looked similarly bruised and battered. But, at least, for the moment they were both still alive.

Ilse had to focus—she knew that much. They, all three, would be the next victims if she didn't find some way to stall. The terror was immense, the horror at what was about to come so crippling she could barely breathe. She'd seen the tortures he'd exacted on his other victims. She could only hope he'd kill the twins quicker if it came to that.

What she assumed was the tip of a knife circled her ear continually, and the voice whispered, "Who should I start with, Ilse Beck? Which of them?"

He knew her name. She frowned, but then realized he must have found her ID in her wallet.

This line of questioning would only lead to violence. So instead, Ilse muttered, "You're not as far ahead as you think. I found you, didn't I?"

He snorted now. Another puff of air against her neck. Ilse closed her own eyes against her pounding headache, trying to focus.

"You found nothing," he snapped. "Luck—luck and nothing more. I led you here. I left the hair. I left the cloth fabric. It was me! You walked right into it."

Ilse paused then shook her head. "You kidnapped adults. This isn't Hansel and Gretel. That's Clyde and Penny. You're a phony."

She wasn't sure this tactic would work. Going on the aggressive would bring pain—she knew that. It came with a sudden slice across her cheek. She yelped, putting her breath into it to give the killer the satisfaction. He wanted to see pain, like any usual sadist, so she gave it to him, acting it up.

Her cheek stung.

But her words also yielded fruit.

"I'm not about to go after kids," he sneered. Now, finally, he stepped into view, like a shadow falling across a visor. He stared down at her, gripping a wickedly curved knife, only slightly less curved than the smile now twisting his features. "You'd like that, wouldn't you? Sicko! I was a kid when I got messed up by ol' mommy. The witch. I leave kids out of it."

Ilse snorted. She knew if she spoke more, it would cause more pain. But this way he wasn't killing anyone. Especially not the twins. So she kept up the aggression, hoping he didn't start cutting rather than slicing. "You failed," she said simply. "You don't know your own stories.

Hansel and Gretel were kids. They left the breadcrumb trail. None of this makes sense. You're just insane. I've seen so many like you it's actually boring at—Agh!"

Her monologue cut off as she felt another sharp slice across her cheek. The knife twisted over her head, and he stood in front of her, panting and staring down at her menacingly. "I'll take your other ear, lady. Don't think I won't. I beat you. I won. You little witch!" he hissed. "I have something special for you. Not a knife. Not this time. You think I don't stick to the story? You'll wish I hadn't, witch lady!"

So that was it. He was bringing her in as another member of the cast in his mind. She wasn't Ilse Beck. She was a stand-in for the witch in the woods.

But how had the witch died...

Ilse paused, and then her eyes widened in horror, flicking to the candlelight sputtering on one of the dusty shelves. Fire. The witch had died of fire.

Shit. Ilse couldn't think of a less desirable way to perish than by flames. Fear came back, trying to burrow into her skull along with the pain. Exhausted, bloody, broken, tired, tied-up, she had every excuse to give in. Every excuse to try and survive, herself.

But Ilse saw that fruit of that choice. She knew the end of that story.

Right now, her life's prospects were grim. But the twins? If she could keep them alive longer, maybe there was a chance someone would find them. She'd tried to call Sawyer twice. The first call had almost connected. The second hadn't gone through at all. She wasn't sure how smartphones worked. Maybe there was a chance he'd see she'd tried to contact him.

Then again, all of this was wishful thinking. Hope buried in hope. But mostly just buried.

She could feel her anger now, too. Not just fear, but rage. She stared at the killer, indifferent to the knife in his hand. "Want to hear a sad truth?" she murmured, her voice hoarse.

He scowled.

She continued, "There are no happy endings. Not for you. Not for people like you. You took the easy road. The only ending you get is disaster. You're not the hero of the story. You're not a storyteller. You're a hack. A monster pretending to be more. You're a sidekick, a secondary character at best. A throwaway redshirt. You're a nothing. You just kill people. It's the easiest thing to do. It makes you nothing!"

He stared at her stunned as if she'd slapped him. After she'd finished, her head still pounding, Ilse felt her mouth go suddenly dry. She just stared at him and realized perhaps she'd pushed a bit *too* hard. Both the twins were looking at her now, panic in their eyes.

She refused to look away, though. Refused to apologize. She gritted her teeth, and through spittle and blood snapped, "You're just like your mother."

This seemed to do it. He howled in rage, eyes blazing. He raised his knife. And so Ilse flung herself forward. Still bound, in the chair, she put her full weight behind the motion. Hitting the ground would hurt. But not before she sent him tumbling.

The killer yelped, reeling back. The twins screamed. Ilse's face hit the dirt painfully, her jaw catching the majority of the impact as her hands were still tied behind her back. The chair pressed uncomfortably against her spine.

A second later, though, as she desperately, breathing dust, tried to twist and see better, she heard a crash.

She tilted her head just enough to glimpse the metal shelf collapse suddenly. The two blazing candles sitting there fell to the wooden floor. The bag of flour, ripped as it was, had caked the lower shelf and part of the floor in a white dust. One of the candles extinguished. But the other, suddenly, hit the flour, which had been disturbed in a puff from the jostled shelves.

The dry, dusty flower suddenly erupted in a fire ball.

The killer howled, stumbling back, batting at his arms which were burning. Ilse desperately tried to rock her hips, to twist her chair over again.

The wooden floors were burning now, too. The dusty bloom of burning flour had quickly caught dried shavings of wood and splinters and old, worn portions of the floor. The flames were spreading. Ilse had hoped to knock the killer into the shelf. Had hoped, even, to knock the candles out.

She hadn't meant to set them all on fire.

Her eyes were so wide they hurt. The killer had doused his sleeve now, smoke rising around him, and he yelped, quickly stepping away from a burning portion of floor.

Just then, above, Ilse heard the sound of rapid footsteps. And a loud voice. "Beck! Doc, you here? Hey! Hey you, down there! Stop!"

Sawyer's voice. Ilse's eyes widened. She screamed, "Here! Tom—it's on fire! He's got a knife!"

The killer howled, lunging towards her. She heard a gunshot above.

And the killer jolted, cursing and stumbling back. He clutched at his arm but retreated out of the sight of the trapdoor in the ceiling. Smoke was rising up now. Flames spread. The twins were mewling desperately, bucking their hips trying to escape the spreading blaze.

The killer clutched a bleeding, gunshot arm, desperate. He stared in horror at the spreading flames. He looked up again towards the trapdoor in the ceiling, a flap of wood dangling within. A figure was moving about above, shouting something into the cellar.

The fire was rising. The shelf with the dusting of flour also erupted into flames. Flames licked at the ceiling now. Covered half the room. Penny's chair was burning. Her fingers were slick and red and she was screaming. "Help! Help! My hand!"

Her brother, spotting this, cursed, ducked his head and slammed his chair into his sister's, sending her toppling away from the flames. But the same motion, brought the large, broad-shouldered youth, crashing to the ground as well, just like Ilse.

The two of them had their faces pressed to the wood, which was quickly going up in smoke. Ash lingered on the air, smoke billowing through the room. Ilse wanted to scream, but now choked on the acrid plumes.

The killer, bleeding, knife in hand, had taken cover against a wall so Sawyer couldn't get an angle on him. And now, in the dark, in the smoke, Ilse lost track of his figure.

"Tom!" she screamed. "To—" but she started hacking and coughing, wheezing. Her face was now warm. Too warm. Sweat didn't come as it dried too quickly. Flames chewed hungrily through the dry floor.

Her face ached. Her shoulder throbbed as she remembered her last experience with fire. That time, a killer had set gasoline off in an apartment. She'd barely escaped then.

But at the time, her hands hadn't been tied.

She spotted a figure suddenly move like a bat through the night, lunging through the smoke towards her. She heard another gunshot. This time, it seemed to miss, but the figure, at the sound of the shot, cursed and lurched back, stumbling. Something fell from his fingers, flashing silver, and hitting the floor.

The knife.

The footsteps above moved now. The killer was cursing, doubled over, searching desperately for his knife. The flames heated Ilse's cheeks, but with a loud groan of effort, she flung herself back. The chair *thumped.* She kicked and flung again. *Another thump.* Like a landed trout flopping on land, she desperately tried to reach the knife.

In the smoke, the confusion, the killer couldn't locate the item.

Ilse's fingers scrambled for the blade, desperately. She had to get free.

"Give me that!" a voice suddenly screamed in her ear. Something slammed against her wrist, trying to break it. She fought, unable to scream from the smoke.

But then, another figure suddenly fell from the ceiling, slamming directly into the killer.

Agent Tom Sawyer had flung himself into a burning room. He landed on the killer, knocking him away from Ilse. The momentum from the fall brought both men to the ground. Sawyer hit the floor with a painful grunt, landing on a patch of fire, but still rolling to try and douse his clothing. The killer crashed back into the metal shelves again, screaming bloody murder.

The twins were still in harm's way. "Sawyer! The kids!" Ilse screamed.

Tom, smoking, singed, got to his feet, whirling about. A cloud of smoke engulfed him. But before he could move, the killer tackled him around the waist, bringing the two of them crashing to the floor. Now, both men were singed. Sawyer's sleeve was on fire. The killer's pant leg was similarly catching blaze.

The twins were screaming for help, desperately trying to free their bonds. Ilse cursed, scrambling desperately with bound hands towards the weapon behind her. Her fingertips grazed the hilt of the blade, scrabbling over the surface. She tried to kick free but failed. She gouged her fingers against the sharp knife and winced but kept at it.

Finally, she maneuvered her hands so that the blade slipped between the palms of her fingers, behind her back. She began worrying at the rope, seething as she moved her hands up and down, desperately.

Sawyer grunted as he caught a blow to the stomach. His arm was still blazing. He shouted in pain but returned a punch of his own, sending smoke swirling and catching the killer in the jaw. The man's head snapped back, and he stumbled away.

Penny was screaming. Ilse worked at the ropes. The fire had spread from the far wall, and now was eating at Penny's chair legs.

Sawyer had the killer's hand gripped in his, holding him and trying to dislodge fingers around his throat. But he heard Penny's cry and turned. With a grunt, he kicked, sending her chair backwards, away from the spreading flames. The killer used the distraction to send a blow into Sawyer's midriff doubling him over. The sandy-haired man let out a long whoosh of air. His baseball hat went flying.

Ilse's hands ripped free. She scrambled to her feet. “Sawyer, run!” she yelled.

She reached the twins' side in rapid pace, dropping by them and working desperately at the ropes. She freed Penny first, who lunged from the chair and sprinted towards concrete steps in the back of the room. She cut the bonds free on Clyde next. The large teen struggled to his feet, limping, burned, smoldering but he also had enough strength to hasten towards the steps.

That's when the ceiling caved in. A burning beam slammed into the ground, cutting off Ilse's view of Sawyer. The fire spread, engulfing the room. She heard screaming, painful shouts.

“Sawyer!” she yelled. She felt hands tugging at her from behind, but she tried to rip free. The hand gripped her though, dragging.

“Come on ma'am,” Clyde's voice shouted in her ear. “Come on!”

She tried to fight but he dragged her back, pulling her to safety. Ilse stared in horror at the burning space.

“Tom!” she screamed. “Tom, get out of there!”

She could no longer see movement. Her eyes stung. Her nostrils ached from the sheer odor of ash. Her cheek was grimy and in pain. Her shoulders were singed. Her sweater still smoking. The moment she hit the concrete stairs, dragged back and up them, she began choking and coughing, gasping at the ground.

A strong handed guided her up, up. Another hand held her on the other side, supporting her. “We've got you, ma'am,” Penny's voice trembled in Ilse's ear. “Thank you. Thank you.”

But Ilse tried with all her might to shove away. Her lips were too dry, too parched, her throat too sore to speak loudly. She tried to protest, to move back down the stairs, but the twins kept shepherding up and away, moving back towards the upper room.

They emerged in the small shed through a sliding panel in one of the walls. A mannequin was knocked to the floor, the head tumbling. Ilse stared in horror at flames eating through the cabin floor as well. The whole thing was going to collapse.

The three of them finally managed to stumble out the door, tripping down wooden steps and collapsing in a three-person heap on the pine-needle strewn ground. Ilse couldn't scream, couldn't speak. Couldn't do much of anything.

Behind her, she spotted flashing lights moving through the trees.

She heard the chatter of voices over the radios. The backup was on its way.

But too late. Far too late.

She stared numbly at the burning cabin, willing herself to rise. She had to go back in and help him. Her legs were weak though. Her head was still pounding horribly. Her heart pattered so rapidly she felt fit to explode.

"Dear God, Tom!" she rasped.

The twins were laying on the ground next to her, both of them sobbing. Ilse heard a voice from the forest suddenly shout. "There! They're up there! Shit—someone call paramedics!"

She heard rapidly pounding footsteps. A figure hastened towards their forms.

Ilse shoved with one hand, but her elbow wouldn't bend. She tried to push up with her other, and this time made it to her knees, but her head pounded, and she lost her balance, collapsing back onto the pine needles.

She felt strong arms at her side now, holding her. "Agent Beck," someone was saying in her ear. "Stay still. Don't move. You're injured."

But Ilse just tried to rise again, rocking on her hips, pushing up. This time she even made it to her feet. She took a wobbly step towards the burning door of the cabin, then collapsed again.

Her head was just spinning too much. Ilse stared towards the doorway, breathing desperately, heart in her throat. Then, she began to drag herself across the detritus-strewn floor. Pulling her body forward once, twice. She heard more radio squawking, more protests from the paramedic next to her.

And then, she went still.

A figure, a shadow was moving inside the smoke, stumbling from the blaze. The figure's shirt was burnt. His left leg was on fire.

The man emerged, blinking wildly, steaming and smoking from every inch. He coughed, gagging and spitting as he stumbled down the steps and hit the ground. For a moment, Ilse didn't recognize him. But then, through a charred, ash-streaked face, two green eyes blinked. A baseball cap, also singed, was gripped tightly in one hand where it had been retrieved from the fire.

She stared. "Tom?" she rasped breathlessly.

The man flashed a thumbs up and then collapsed, gasping at the sky, heaving a long breath that puffed a geyser of smoke towards the stars.

Only then, seeing Sawyer lying there, motionless, did Ilse finally allow her own eyes to close.

"Paramedics!" someone was still screaming. "More—yes, there. All four. Yes, found them. Sir—yes, sir? No. Everyone. They're here. All of them—yes, I'm sure."

The radio chatter, the shouts and calls, faded slowly in Ilse's mind. She blinked a couple of times but could no longer see. Even the pain in her head, along her arm and shoulders and cheek started to fade.

She smiled as she listened to the twins both trying to speak.

They lived. They'd survived.

Thank God.

CHAPTER TWENTY EIGHT

Tom wasn't sure how often he'd end up in a hospital, watching Ilse Beck sleep. She looked so peaceful on the hospital bed, on the other side of the privacy curtain between their rooms. She had bandages on her cheek and head. More bandages along her arm. Thankfully, Ilse's burns, unlike his, hadn't been too severe.

Sawyer glanced towards his shooting hand, wincing. The worst of his burns had been along the back of his right hand. His shooting hand. There'd been talk of amputating the damn thing, but Sawyer had refused. Well, more accurately, he'd threatened to kill the doctor in his sleep if he even tried it.

The pain along his arm, and up and down his leg was immense. It had been touch-and-go at first, but now the doctors said his skin should heal.

The same, of course, couldn't be said for Guy Wolfe. The man was now toast, burnt to a crisp. They'd found his remains and matched them with the DNA of the hair.

Sawyer winced, leaning back in his cot, propped up, his bandaged arm resting against his chest. He watched Ilse sleep, frowning to himself. She looked peaceful lying there, but he'd seen something different back in that forest. She'd been brave. Courageous. But he'd seen fear in her eyes. A terror so deep it had taken his breath away. He'd seen it before, but never for such a long period of time.

Dr. Beck wasn't like most people. She had demons of her own to worry about. Perhaps he'd misjudged her. Maybe, if there was someone who could be trusted with Rebekah's story, it was Ilse.

Regardless, he'd already made up his mind. No matter what, he wasn't going to tell her about his plan for revenge. One benefit of spending a week in the hospital, it gave him ample time to think. And now, as he lay there, he allowed himself a grim nod of satisfaction. He knew how he would get his sister's killer. He now had a plan. A job like this didn't always guarantee old age. Which meant he had to act while he still could.

He let out a slow, painful breath, twisting his head faintly, adjusting his bandaged hand and closing his eyes.

Dr. Beck could be trusted. She had demons of her own haunting her. But at the end of the day, only one person would put Rebekah's killer in the ground. He refused to get anyone else involved.

"Tom?" Ilse's voice came soft and faint.

He remained in his bed, eyes closed now. For a moment, he wanted to say something. They'd made a good team back there. Ilse had a way of zoning in on their suspects' motives. And Sawyer had a way of not getting too caught up in the emotional side of things. He caught them. End of story.

He let out a faint little breath, but kept his eyes closed. He didn't like talking much anyway. Besides, there would be plenty of time for talking later.

***

After eight days in the hospital, Ilse was finally glad to be home. She sat in front of her computer on the borrowed web cam, smiling politely towards a client displayed on the computer screen. She waited a moment, then nodded. "Alright then, I'll see you next week, okay?"

Ilse wore a windbreaker instead of her usual sweater. She didn't want to alarm her clients with the bandages along her arm and back. The stitches on her head, though, were healing nicely and hidden mostly by the hair now regrowing over her ear. The cuts on her cheek hadn't been deep enough to leave scars.

Ilse gave a final salute of farewell to her client, then signed off, sighing in contentment at a session gone well. She glanced towards the small, wooden carved figure she'd found on her hospital bed the day before she'd left. She smiled. A tiny, little wooden fairy. Like from a story book. Sawyer had whittled it for her.

It was his version of a long conversation, a hug and a reluctant apology, rolled in one. She touched the sanded surface of the wooden fairy and smiled again.

She sat in her chair for a moment, glad to be back at her apartment. But another part of her was distracted. She glanced towards the pile of mail she'd brought in just before the session had begun. She hadn't had time to go through it. But she had spotted the postcard hidden amid the bills and advertisements.

Ilse let out a faint puff, glancing towards the pile of mail now, and frowning to herself.

The hospital had been a nice reprieve from her daily duties. Not only that, it had given her a momentary respite from the haunting of postcards and contact information. Whoever was still hounding her, be it her father or his mistress, they were clearly insistent.

Ilse had even changed the locks on her door.

She pushed slowly to her feet, wincing as she did and touching gingerly to the stitches above her ear. She then moved towards the door, coughing occasionally as she did. The cough, according to the doctors, was caused by damage from the fire. She would make a recovery, but it would take a bit more time.

Ilse paused over the pile of discarded mail where she'd left it. A hanging brochure for a nearby carwash half obscured the postcard.

But with a faint sigh of resignation, frowning, she bent over, picking up the card. This time, the image was a custom one. Someone had taken a photograph of her apartment and created it into a postcard. Ilse felt a flicker of anxiety.

How had they gotten a photograph of her apartment? From the real estate website online?

Or... or in person?

She felt a slow shiver turn to dread. She turned the card over, with almost an air of inevitability.

And there, on the back, she spotted a single sentence. *"Naughty Tom Sawyer burned that man... Shame."*

Ilse just stared, her heart in her throat. How could her father, back in prison, possibly know about Tom? How could they have a picture of her apartment?

She stomped over to the window, gripping the postcard in a trembling fist. She stared out at the street, her eyes searching for... for something.

But passing traffic, pedestrians, store fronts across the street—none of it stood out as untoward.

She looked back at the taunting letter, feeling her anger returning now like a cold prickle. With a growl, she slowly crumpled the thing. But this wasn't enough. She marched back towards the kitchen, looking for matches.

Ilse's hands shook as she grabbed a match above her wood burning stove, tossed the note card in the sink then lit it.

She stared at the fire, watching the card incinerate against the steel basin.

As she stood there, her eyes flickering with the flames in the sink, she felt a cold, dreadful certainty.

Her father wasn't the one sending her the notes.

It wasn't possible. He wouldn't have known about Sawyer. He couldn't have taken the photos of her apartment.

The mistress? Had the woman followed Ilse back from Barcelona? Or was she just overthinking it?

Ilse shivered, holding her hands around her arms, wrapping tight. The slow trail of smoke lifted from the note card and she turned on the faucets, dousing the thing before it set the alarms off.

As she stood there, inhaling the faint scent of smoke... Her phone began to ring.

Ilse hesitated, swallowing slowly. She lifted the device, frowning at the unknown number. A second passed, then she answered. "H-hello? Who is this?"

A voice breathed on the other end. "Your father is up for parole," the voice said simply. A feminine voice? No... Well, perhaps. Was it muffled? "Just thought you'd want to know."

Then, the call ended.

Ilse stood in her small apartment kitchen, exhaling slowly. Parole? Was it possible? Was Gerald Mueller up for release?

She stared at her computer screen, wondering if she ought to look it up.

Her father wasn't sending her the postcards. So who had just called her?

She scowled, lifting the phone and trying to dial the number back. But instantly she was met by a disconnected tone.

"Dammit," she growled, wincing as she moved her head but bunching a hand at her side. "Damn it!" she repeated, louder, scooping her hand into the sink and ripping the wet residue of burnt paper before flinging it into the trash can beneath the sink.

That's what she thought of those postcards. That's what she thought of anonymous tips. And that, most of all, was what she thought of the prospect of her own father being released from prison. He'd never been indited for the actual murders, only the child abuse.

Who was taunting her? What role was her father playing in all of this?

With a faint sigh, Ilse tried to compose herself. She breathed slowly, raised her phone, dialing a new number. After the second ring, they answered.

"Hey, Rudy," Ilse said slowly. "I need you to look something up for me. No, no, Sawyer's not here. Please. I'd owe you one." She inhaled shakily, standing by the sink, her fingers stained in ash and slick with water droplets. "Please," she said slowly. "I need you to see if a man named Gerald Mueller is up for parole. He's in prison in Germany. Do you think you can do that?" She hesitated again, listening to the response. Then said, in a hoarse tone. "And Rudy, you have to swear to me, this is our secret. Got it? You can't tell *anyone.*"

EPILOGUE

His bones were so very cold. No matter how many times he wrapped himself in layers, jackets, even coats, he never could get warm. He stood on his porch, an oversized winter jacket hugging his thin frame. His legs looked so small compared to his upper torso, wrapped in two sweaters, two shirts, and his coat.

But he didn't care how he looked. He didn't much leave his home anyway. Not unless it was for a special occasion.

He glanced towards his phone, studying the video feed there.

Notification bubbles popped at the top of the screen and he frowned towards these, tilting his head. Anything in the news about Ilse Beck, Tom Sawyer, or Gerald Mueller would *ding* on his phone. A constant stream of data and information.

"Will she sleep?" he murmured to himself.

He nodded at his own question. In a faint, feminine voice, he replied. "She will sleep, my sweet."

He gave himself a faint pat on the chest, rubbing his fingers in circles against his coat in an affectionate motion. He ran fingers through his shoulder length hair, brushing it past his ears. He had dark hair, just like Dr. Beck did. It was one of the points they'd connected on all those years ago.

Of course, all good things came to an end.

There had been other... differences they hadn't connected on.

"She was my patient, though, wasn't she?" he hissed to himself.

Just as quickly he bobbed his head, snapping his fingers. "Yes. Yes she was. What a shitty thing to do. She deserves it."

He winced, shaking his head, and leaning back against the glass of his patio. "Does she?" he whispered. "It is somewhat cruel. Isn't it?"

But he snorted in derision, slapping himself across the cheek. "Don't be a fool," he snapped. "She has done worse, hasn't she? She ruined *our patient.* How dare she?"

He sighed, nodding slowly. He hated when he got like this. It was difficult to break the mood. He'd managed to keep himself in check, only sending the postcards. Not just that, though...

He turned back, wincing and stepping into the house.

The far wall was plastered with photos, articles, case reports. All of them on Dr. Ilse Beck. A headshot, blown up to the size of his TV, centered it all.

He glared at Ilse's face, gritting his teeth as he stared.

She thought she knew better than everyone. Hadn't seen fitting to leave well enough alone. And so she'd meddled where she wasn't wanted. She'd taken something very dear from him.

And so he would take something back.

Well... more accurately, *she* would.

He smiled at the thought now, tracing his fingers over one of the smaller, candid phots he had of the woman. This photo had been taken through the blinds at her apartment when she'd been getting dressed. She hadn't noticed a thing.

His fingers lingered against the smooth surface of the picture.

He licked his lips faintly and murmured. "No... no we won't take anything, will we?"

He smirked. In that softer voice he said, "She will. She'll do it. We both know she will. We *know Ilse Beck.*"

Indeed, they did. They'd spent years researching every single thing about her. Where she'd gone to school, who her favorite teachers had been, who her first clients had been. Her favorite food. He knew she practiced jujitsu, knew she'd been a runner in school. Knew her favorite color was black, like the sweaters she wore.

He knew everything there was to know.

All of it, of course, had an end in sight.

He removed his finger slowly from the glossy photo, scowling at it. She was smiling in the photo, or, at least, seemed to be. Perhaps she was on a phone call with that FBI agent she fancied. Tom Sawyer. What a silly name. He stared at the candid photo of his target. She didn't deserve to be happy. He was going to great lengths to make sure she *wasn't* happy. That was only the start, though. He would take her happiness, and then she would do the rest.

With another long look at the smiling face in the photo, he pulled the picture from the wall and tore it in two.

He wouldn't kill her. That would defeat the point. She was the taker after all. She'd been the one to steal from him.

And so now, he would push her to the edge. He would make *her* take her own life.

He nodded to himself in satisfaction and then let go of the shredded postcard, watching as the two halves tumbled to the ground.

NOW AVAILABLE!

NOT LIKE BEFORE
(An Ilse Beck FBI Suspense Thriller—Book 6)

Victims are going missing, clearly victims of a serial killer, and FBI Special Agent Ilse Beck suspects this is no ordinary killer—with no ordinary M.O. With the clock running out, can she crack the case in time to save the next victim?

In this bestselling mystery series, FBI Special Agent Ilse Beck, victim of a traumatic childhood in Germany, moved to the U.S. to become a renowned psychologist specializing in PTSD, and the world's leading expert in the unique trauma of serial-killer survivors. By studying the psychology of their survivors, Ilse has a unique and unparalleled expertise in the true psychology of serial killers. Ilse never expected, though, to become an FBI agent herself.

As Ilse goes deeper down the rabbit hole, she soon realizes something isn't adding up. She must put her brilliant mind to the test to make sense of all the evidence—including the clues that may be hiding right under her nose.

Will she crack under the pressure?

And will it be too late?

A dark and suspenseful crime thriller, the bestselling ILSE BECK series is a breathtaking page-turner, an unputdownable mystery and suspense novel. A compelling and perplexing psychological thriller, rife with twists and jaw-dropping secrets, it will make you fall in love with a brilliant new female protagonist, while it keeps you shocked late into the night.

NOT LIKE BEFORE (An Ilse Beck FBI Suspense Thriller) is book #6 in a new series by bestselling mystery and suspense author Ava Strong.

Book #7—NOT LIKE NORMAL—is also available.

Ava Strong

Debut author Ava Strong is author of the REMI LAURENT mystery series, comprising six books (and counting); of the ILSE BECK mystery series, comprising seven books (and counting); of the STELLA FALL psychological suspense thriller series, comprising six books (and counting); and of the DAKOTA STEELE FBI suspense thriller series, comprising three books (and counting).

An avid reader and lifelong fan of the mystery and thriller genres, Ava loves to hear from you, so please feel free to visit www.avastrongauthor.com to learn more and stay in touch.

BOOKS BY AVA STRONG

REMI LAURENT FBI SUSPENSE THRILLER
THE DEATH CODE (Book #1)
THE MURDER CODE (Book #2)
THE MALICE CODE (Book #3)
THE VENGEANCE CODE (Book #4)
THE DECEPTION CODE (Book #5)
THE SEDUCTION CODE (Book #6)

ILSE BECK FBI SUSPENSE THRILLER
NOT LIKE US (Book #1)
NOT LIKE HE SEEMED (Book #2)
NOT LIKE YESTERDAY (Book #3)
NOT LIKE THIS (Book #4)
NOT LIKE SHE THOUGHT (Book #5)
NOT LIKE BEFORE (Book #6)
NOT LIKE NORMAL (Book #7)

STELLA FALL PSYCHOLOGICAL SUSPENSE THRILLER
HIS OTHER WIFE (Book #1)
HIS OTHER LIE (Book #2)
HIS OTHER SECRET (Book #3)
HIS OTHER MISTRESS (Book #4)
HIS OTHER LIFE (Book #5)
HIS OTHER TRUTH (Book #6)

DAKOTA STEELE FBI SUSPENSE THRILLER
WITHOUT MERCY (Book #1)
WITHOUT REMORSE (Book #2)
WITHOUT A PAST (Book #3)

www.ingramcontent.com/pod-product-compliance
Lightning Source LLC
Chambersburg PA
CBHW030615310726
48979CB00003B/727

* 9 7 8 1 0 9 4 3 9 4 1 8 3 *